Double Stuffed

By Sylvia Morrow

Content Notes

This book is intended for adults only. There will be sexual and violent situations, just like there were in the first book in the series. For more detailed content notes please see the author's website at SylviaMorrow.com. There are things that some readers may not be comfortable with and it's important that everyone watch out for their own mental health.

This is the sequel to a book called "Stuffed" and it is highly recommended that you read the first book before reading this one.

CHAPTER ONE

Ori

"Carl," I say to our goldfish. "Prepare yourself for a night of having to listen to loud and boisterous intercourse. Louder than usual, I should say."

My Anne. My darling Anne. She'll be home soon, and I can tell her of the wonderful thing I've discovered. Oh, how excited she'll be. I'm certain of it.

I brush my shoulders off and smirk. Anne and I have had a wonderful relationship these past few months and we've kept things quite lively in the bedroom. I'll do whatever it takes to please my Anne.

The lock on the door clicks as a key turns inside it. She's home! My love! I stand near the door, next to Carl, waiting as I do each day for her when she comes home from work. The door opens and there she is. Her short brown hair is mussed, her eyes sleepy, even her glasses are a little crooked as if too tired to stay on straight. It's clear she's exhausted. I probably should let her rest before pouncing on her, but I can't keep this exciting news inside.

"Welcome home darling." I kiss her soft cheek, my feather-filled body nearly bursting at the seams with excitement. "I have wonderful news."

"Hi Ori," she says with a yawn, then turns to Carl and waves at his tank. "Hello Carl, sweetie. Alright Ori, can the news wait until after I have a shower?"

"I'll be quick," I reply, bouncing on my toes. "I found the most exciting thing on the internet today."

"Oh boy." Anne rubs her temples and sits on the sofa.

"I swear it's good. I promise I'm not being scammed or fooled by a creepypasta yet again."

I cringe a little as I recall the times my naivety got me in trouble. Oh well, that's the past. This is the wonderful future.

"No this, my love, is fantastic."

I drop to my knees before her and take hold of her hands. Anne flinches—she must be thinking about how many germs are on her hands right now, and that I'm touching them. We've been working on that, however—her problems with germs—-and she knows rationally all will be fine in a moment. She takes a calming breath. When she relaxes after only a second, I continue.

"Anne. I've discovered something we can explore together. I think you'll love it. It's called —" I pause dramatically as I rise, take hold of her face, and look her directly in the eyes, "—the Omegaverse."

Anne stays silent for a long moment, only blinking. She suddenly breaks out into wild laughter. Confusion crosses my face. I set my hands in my lap and settle to the floor. *Why is she laughing? This is a serious matter.*

"Oh, Ori. You're so sweet. I'll get in the shower, clean up, and we can talk after. I have some stuff we need to talk about anyway, okay? We can talk about your..." she breaks out into giggles for a moment again before continuing, "*discovery* in a bit."

Disappointed but relieved that we'll still address it, I stand to assist Anne in rising from the sofa. She's so beautiful and perfect I can't help but agree to anything she asks. She's the reason I'm alive, after all.

"Alright, darling. Shall I join you?"

Her gaze heats as she inspects my form. I watch as her breathing increases in speed and her pupils dilate. *Yes. There she is, my spicy girl.*

"You'll get all soggy. You're made of fabric. Won't that be an issue?" she asks in a near whisper.

"You know I clean and dry myself carefully in private. I can handle it. I'll stay mostly out of the spray. Let me wash you."

As long as I'm careful not to get *too* wet.

Taking her hips, I press them against me so that she can feel how hard I am for her. She moans and grinds her pelvis harder against me. Our desire for one another has not lessened one bit over time.

"I take my washing very seriously."

"No one takes anything as seriously as I take pleasuring you, Anne," I tell her, and *I mean it with everything I am.*

Anne whimpers as I lift her and carry her to the bathroom. I set her on the edge of the far side of the bath while I run the water, testing it with one finger to make sure the temperature is right. When it's ready, I undress, as does my Anne. I open the curtain, ready to properly welcome her home.

CHAPTER TWO

Anne

"Oh, Ori, that feels amazing," I moan as he runs the loofah up and down my back.

The scent of the antibacterial soap relaxes me after a hard day at work, and the scratch of the loofah makes me feel like all my troubles are being scrubbed away.

Only lightly damp, Ori has managed to stay out of the spray. When I turn around, he still looks just as gorgeous as always. His black hair sticks to his forehead from the steam and I reach up to smooth it back. Ori takes hold of my waist, pressing me tightly against him.

"Nothing could feel as good as your skin against mine, Anne." Ori bathes me in compliments as well as water. "Nothing except the way it feels to be inside you, of course."

His gaze lowers to my lips. My stomach flutters with delight at the impending kiss. I will never, ever tire of this man. The water sprays over my back, hot and stinging the way I like it, as he leans in for a kiss...until his hands slip off my waist. Ori steps back and raises his arms with a frown.

"Damn," he says as he inspects the soggy clumps at the ends of his wrists that were his hands. "I held them too long in the water. Help me wring them out, will you?"

Ori grimaces with embarrassment and my heart aches for him. The poor guy has a lot of troubles due to him being made of fabric and feathers.

"Of course I'll help you, honey." I wring one hand out, then the other.

Ori steps out of the shower, carefully avoiding the spray, and shakes off his hands until they're more or less back into shape. Then, with a focused look on his face, he puffs them properly back up.

"There we are. Should be fine in a moment. No harm done, aside from the temporary wrinkles. A quick blow-dry should smooth those out. I'll stand here and dry off while you finish your shower, darling. Then we can dress and have our discussion."

"And dinner. I'm starving."

As if on cue my stomach rumbles.

I hurry to rinse shampoo from my hair. "Do you know if we have any more leftover pizza? I'm too tired to cook, ugh."

"Well, neither Carl nor I ate it, so if you didn't, then it should still be there."

"Oh, good point," I say with a laugh. "Leftover pizza and a chat it is."

A few minutes later, we're snuggled together on the sofa in pajamas while I eat my reheated pizza, a boy band playing in the background. Ori reads something on the phone I bought him with a confused look.

"I still don't understand. Is it 'Boys' or 'Boy Scouts'? And what does 'Bulletproof' have to do with anything?"

I swallow my pepperoni and sigh. "Once again, I don't know. I'm not Army or whatever, I'm just a casual listener. Okay, one more bite, then I'm done."

With the last bite, I stand and walk to the kitchen. Giving the plate a wash, I then put it into the dishwasher. I like to clean my dishes thoroughly before washing and use the dishwasher to dry them as hot as possible. You can never be too careful with food safety. When I make it back to Ori, his phone is put away while he sits peacefully, watching Carl swim around. No one can sit as quietly and peacefully for as long as Ori; he had a ton of practice when he was a pillow.

I curl up next to him and snuggle under his arm, which he wraps around me. "Alright, I think we need to discuss something pretty important, Ori."

"Yes. The Omegaverse is quite exciting. We don't have a beta, but I think we'll be fine. Of course, I'll be the alpha, and-"

"Ori!" I interrupt. "That's not what I meant. We can talk about that later if you still want to. Though honestly you really should get off those fan fiction websites for a bit. I never spent as much time on them as you do even in my high school days. And anyway, what I need to say is about our daily life, not just the bedroom stuff."

"Oh, alright then. Go on, little omega." He pats me on the head, and I give him a dry look before continuing.

"I think it's time you get out of the house. Every day I go to work, and you stay home and it's not really any kind of life for you. I know I have my own problems, but I can't let them get in the way of you exploring the world. So, I need to be strong for both of us and work through my shit." I sit up straight and give Ori a determined look. "Ori. We're going to the mall."

"But you hate the mall. You've said so several times when your mother tried to get you to go with her," Ori replies, eyebrows raised in shock.

He hasn't met my mom yet, but he's overheard plenty of the conversations between her and I.

"I know I do."

"Even when I told you that millennials statistically have a fondness for malls and want to see them return to their glory days you still-"

"Ori, I know. I remember. This is an example of you being home too much. You sat on the computer and looked up statistics about millennials and their shopping habits when you don't even shop. You should be out experiencing these things, not just reading about them. Don't you want to?" I plead.

Ori gives me a soft look and runs his hand along my jaw. "Of course, I want to, my love. I simply don't want to make you do anything you don't want to. If it pleased you, I would remain inside forever. It's not as if I know the difference anyway. The only other places I've been, besides our Sunday walks to the park, are the animal rescue down the street and the lingerie store two blocks away. I quite liked that place, by the way. We should go again soon."

My cheeks turn red as I roll my eyes. He liked the lingerie place *a lot* indeed. We spent all of my birthday money there, in fact. And *wow* was it worth every penny.

"Honey, I don't want you to be stuck anywhere. It's time you stopped living only for me. You deserve to find something else that you love. And before you say something incredibly sweet, like I know you were about to, I know you'll never love anything as much as me. But you don't have to. You just have to find something you really care about."

He crosses his arms and gives me a grumpy look. "I care about things."

"Like what?"

"Like…Carl. I care a lot about Carl. His whole life depends on me, in fact, and I take very good care of him." He smooths the front of his shirt and straightens his posture.

"Yes, you do. I love Carl too. But I mean something outside of the house."

Ori slumps again. "Fine. I suppose I'm a little nervous. I don't want anything to happen that could get me taken from you. People would see me as a monster, you know. They'd study me in a lab. Take me apart. I'd never see you again if they found me out, Anne."

"We won't let them discover your secrets then, Ori. You forget that I love you just as much as you love me."

"Impossible." He scoffs.

"Hey! I took *seven* of your tentacles at once last night. If that's not love, I don't know what is."

Ori offers me a lascivious grin. "It was eight, Anne. If you lost count so easily, it wasn't enough."

I clear my throat as my cheeks heat. "Anyway, the mall. I think it's a good place to start because it has a lot of sensory experiences and different types of people. Plus, it will be good practice for me since I need to get used to loud sounds again. Any time I have to deal with them at work I just get overwhelmed and exhausted. And the mall is close, so if things get tough it's only one short bus ride home."

"We should get a car." Ori frowns. "We could make a better escape if things went south."

"If you want a car, you better get a job," I grumble.

Ori grins. "Well, as your alpha I am meant to be the provider of the family so I suppose I should seek employment soon."

"Oh, boy."

CHAPTER THREE
Ori

Halloween. Anne insists we practice dealing with the public before our mall trip, doing so while still at home is a perfect idea. This means standing on the outside stairs, handing out candy to *children* while in *costume*.

The costume part is mildly entertaining, I suppose. I've been Anne's "butler" all along and it's nice to switch things up for a night. It's quite simple for me to get into costume, as I can change appearance at will. It does take a bit of power, however. Thankfully, on our walk last Sunday someone was harassing an elderly woman ahead of us. I took a few sips from the hooligan as we passed them by without Anne noticing. We did have to purchase some bits of the costume though, since I couldn't produce the accessories myself. I'm not enjoying wearing them.

"Must I wear this mask?" I ask, adjusting it once more.

The white mask only covers my eyes, yes, but it's quite annoying. I prefer to have my vision unobstructed in every direction so that I may be on guard to protect Anne all the better.

"If you don't wear both the tuxedo and the mask the costume won't make sense. If I can deal with this ultra long, itchy, blonde wig all evening then you can deal with a little mask."

"It's not the same." I take hold of the cauldron of candy we have prepared for the neighborhood children in my white-gloved hands and stand next to Carl's tank. "Did I tell you that you look lovely?"

"Only about a million times," Anne laughs. "But I love hearing it each time."

"Good. Because I love saying it. What panties are you wearing under that tiny blue skirt, by the way? So that I can at least think about tearing them off while I do this terrible chore."

"You're a pervert. Did you know that?" she scoffs.

"Yes. Now answer the question."

"The white ones with the ruffles." She bites her lip and runs her gloved hand down my white vest. She knows very well that those are my favorite.

"I'm going to take those off with my teeth, you tease," I growl, clutching the cauldron tightly.

"It'll have to wait until I get my treat. I plan on sucking on my candy as soon as we're back inside." She walks past me to the door, stroking my cheek as she goes.

"Tease. Horrible woman."

"You'll just have to punish me for it later then, won't you?" she asks as she opens the door, walking out with an extra sway to her full hips, the red bow at the back of her skirt shaking with each step.

"I certainly will," I whisper, following her out the door and locking it behind us.

Passing out the candy is...fine. I mostly sit on the stairs and hold the cauldron. Anne stands a couple steps above me, waving and talking to anyone that says anything to us. I admit that some of the children are...cute. I even decide that I don't dislike *all* children. Anne tells me she feels the same, though she still does not want them to touch her. They're too *sticky* and full of *germs, she* says. Seeing all the leaky noses, I can't say she's wrong.

When the stream of children comes to an end, Anne stretches out her arms and her white-booted legs with a long yawn.

"I think it's finally time to go in and take a long shower. I did pretty well, though, didn't I?"

She smiles proudly.

"Yes, you did, darling. You did wonderfully. I'm ready to go home as well." I smile as sweetly, hiding how ready I am to ravish her as soon as our door closes.

And I do. Once we're inside, I toss the cauldron down, creating a loud clatter that startles Anne. Wide-eyed, she looks at me, searching for something wrong, a reason why I tossed it so suddenly. Nothing wrong at all.

"On your knees," I command.

I fling the horrid mask across the room. Once the cape that has been annoying me all night is untied, I let it fall to the floor. "We're going to have to take that wig off darling, there's no way it's going to withstand this."

"What's all this about?" Anne asks, eyes wide.

Hand on her chest, she plays at being shocked by my demands. I love my naughty little actress oh so much.

"I told you I'd punish you, my love."

"In the name of the moon?" she asks with a cheeky grin, pointing to her costume.

I roll my eyes with a huff. "We can do this

the hard way, if you like."

Stroking her cheek with the back of my hand allows me the privilege of watching her eyes flutter closed in an uncharacteristically angelic way. When her lips turn up in a softly relaxed smile, I take my moment to strike. Lifting her over my shoulder, I carry her to the kitchen.

"Hey! What are you doing?" she laughs.

"Punishing a brat."

I lay her back first on the kitchen table and spin her toward me, so that her head hangs over the edge, looking up at me. When she tries to sit up, I gently press her back down. As I undo my pants, her eyes widen again, this time in genuine surprise.

"Oh," she breathes out, "I see."

"Now, open very, very wide."

Licking her lips with a grin she lets out one breathy laugh before following my instructions. I slide my fabric cock into her soft, wet mouth with a sigh that speaks more words than I could say. The first bit of drool at the corner of her lips brings a dark chuckle from the depths of my cotton chest.

"That's my Anne. My naughty, darling Anne."

The wig very much does not withstand this.

CHAPTER FOUR
Anne

My yellow-blonde wig falls to the floor as Ori's wonderfully non-flesh cock pushes hard into the back of my throat, making me gag. I relax and let him pass deeper. While he fucks my mouth, I reach between my legs and rub my clit in quick circles.

I love that Ori can be so commanding like this sometimes, but so sweet and giving others. He always seems to know what I want before I even do. I mean, I certainly didn't know I wanted to be face-fucked on the kitchen table tonight, that's for sure.

"You look so lovely with my cock in your mouth. You're taking me so well, Anne."

His words make me moan around the thickness of him. I rub myself faster. I love it when he talks like that. That's just the thing; he's never really cruel. The last three months we've done a lot, like *a lot,* of experimenting and discovered what we like. And so maybe I like just a little punishment mixed with all the praise he loves giving me. He's all too happy to oblige. It's just another way we're perfect for each other.

He thrusts into me faster. I feel myself approaching climax already. My fingers are drenched and sliding around in firm, manic circles as I get closer and closer to my finish.

"Your punishment is nearly at an end. You're such a good girl."

He's panting now and his thrusts are losing their rhythm. He's almost there.

My hips begin to raise, my thighs tightening. A strong orgasm crashes through me at the same time as Ori pulls out of my mouth. My pussy flutters as I hear the sloppy wetness of my saliva on him. He pumps himself once, twice, and groans.

Feathers fall over my face and chest. I sneeze as they tickle my nose, sputtering as I try to spit one out that's stuck to my tongue. Ori helps me sit, brushing feathers off as he does so.

"You did so well, my love. Thank you."

"Yeah, well, you have to clean up the feathers."

"I always do." He kisses the side of my head and takes my hands in his. "Now, I know you want to take your shower, so why don't you do that, and I'll clean up and make dinner."

"You're a wonderful househusband, you know that?" I ask with a laugh.

"Only an alpha providing sustenance for my omega." He gently slaps me on the ass as I walk away.

"You're so weird," I shout behind me as I walk to the bathroom.

"I'm literally a pillow. What do you expect?"

"He's right, I guess," I laugh to myself.

My shower is hot and brief but sufficient. I put on clean, soft pajamas and find Ori already at the stove making me a grilled cheese and tomato soup.

"Sorry for the simple fare. It's quite late and I didn't want to make something that took all night. I know you have a meeting in the morning."

"Oh, Ori. It's wonderful."

How many guys would be as considerate and sweet as he is? Yeah, okay, he's only cleaning the house, making dinner, and remembering my work schedule. But that's on top of all the other little things he does every day. And I know he would do *anything* for me. I'm so lucky to have him. I doubt there could ever be a second guy as good as Ori on the entire planet.

We eat dinner—well I eat. Ori tells me about a game he played while I was at work, and then we make plans for our trip to the mall. I'm excited for Ori to explore more of the world than he has so far, but I admit I'm not particularly excited about leaving the house myself. I've had bad luck with people in my life so far and have no reason to believe this time will be better than any other. But, if Ori will do anything for me, I'll do anything for him.

"Oh, we can't forget to feed Carl," I say as we're about to head off to bed.

"Oh dear, I almost did forget in my excitement." Ori bends down to Carl's level with a frown. "Apologies, my friend."

Ori and I grab some blood worms for Carl in honor of the spooky holiday and drop them into his tank.

"Goodnight Carl," we say together before heading off to bed.

Time to get some sleep. I have a busy day tomorrow. Then, the day after that is my adventure with the best man in the world.

CHAPTER FIVE
Ori

Ugh. *The bus.* I shield Anne with my jacket the whole ride to the mall. She's taken the day off of work so that we may go at a time of day when it won't be busy. So smart, she is. My darling Anne.

Ding

The bus arrives at our stop, and we wait for the last person to exit before we do. Thankfully we avoid getting shoved or otherwise jostled about. It would be a shame to start this trip off with Anne in a panic. As it is, she's already rubbing her fingertips together in the way she does when she's nervous or stressed. I take her hand in mine and smile down at her.

"It will be alright. Now, show me the mall. I need to understand this important cultural gathering space. Perhaps then I'll learn enough about social skills to be able to get a job."

"Important cultural gathering space? If you say so." She squeezes my hand and smiles up at me. "Okay. Let's go. I want a soft pretzel and a smoothie."

"What good will *you* getting food teach *me*?" I gripe as she tugs me along behind her.

"It will teach you the difference between a hangry Anne and a happy Anne."

"Oh, I know that one already. I was pretty sure you were going to take a bite out of my arm last Tuesday when we were waiting for the pizza to be delivered." I chuckle at the memory.

"I wasn't far off. Okay, here we are. The mall!" Anne opens the glass doors, and we walk into a larger building than I could have imagined.

Of course, I've seen massive structures on the television and such but to be *inside* one is entirely different. In fact, it's overwhelming and I take a step toward the walls to ground myself.

"Ori, are you ok? You don't look so good," Anne asks with pinched brows.

"I'm fine," I stammer out. "It's just so...a lot."

Anne looks around us, taking in everything before returning her attention to me. "Yep. I guess. It's not really that big of a mall. I've been to the biggest mall in the country before and that one is, like, *really* overwhelming. It even has a rollercoaster inside!"

"I will not be riding a rollercoaster. I don't know what would happen to me," I insist.

"Don't worry, there's no rollercoaster here. This mall is barely big enough to have a movie theater next to it. It's fine."

"Alright. Lead me to your pretzel, then." I hold out my hand and this time, she's the one in front when we start walking.

The pretzel stand is near the entrance. It takes only a moment waiting in line. I proudly pay the man at the register like I learned how to do on our trip to the lingerie store—though of course I must use Anne's money to do so. The smoothie bar is next to the pretzel stand. Ordering there goes just as smoothly, though the sound of the blender aggravates Anne's anxiety.

We sit on a bench and Anne smothers her hands in hand sanitizer several times before she eats. I'm proud of her for eating in a place where she's unable to properly wash her hands, even if it means she goes a touch overboard with the precautions. She's taking big steps today.

I watch her quietly as she eats. Smiling, she chews and looks around at the shops near us and all the things in the windows. There are few people here at this time of day to upset her. I've never seen her out like this. It's a wonderful sight. If I could, I would kiss her right here, make love to her on this bench in the wide-open space of this community landmark. But that will have to wait.

She finishes her smoothie and looks over at my silent face. "What? You're being so quiet."

"You're just so perfect. I didn't want to interrupt."

"Oh jeez. You're so sweet. Okay, let's get up. Where should we go first? I say not the fancy candle store."

We both look at the scented candle store across from us. The thought of flames on fabric crosses my mind, making me shudder.

"No candles."

"We already had food so let's avoid any restaurants or treat shops for now. You already make your own clothes. Hmm. Let's just get up and walk around, see what looks fun."

Strolling along the long halls of the mall with Anne's hand in mine fills me with pride. The people passing by feel like my subjects and I their king when I have such a majestic queen as her on my arm. The air is fragrant with so many scents, such as the terrifying candle shop, a cinnamon roll stand Anne says we should stop at later, a perfume kiosk. The colors and lights are bright and vibrant —I don't know where to settle my eyes. A glowing red sign for the exit, a bright yellow sign above a shoe store, bright purple letters announcing a doll crafting business.

Wait. This doll crafting place. "Make-A-Friend", it's called. I pause in front of it and stare into the large glass front of the store, watching the employees do their work.

"Anne," I say, completely mesmerized by the sight before me. "We must go inside."

My Anne furrows her brow as she peers into the window, then turns back to me. "You want to make a stuffed animal?"

"Absolutely."

"Are you sure? They're kind of expensive so if you don't really want one-"

"I want one."

"Okay then. Make-A-Friend it is."

The store is mostly empty at this time of day, with the children who would normally be occupying it at school and their parents at work. The lighting is bright, the atmosphere cheerful, every employee with a smile on their face. Sighing with happiness, I walk to one employee who greets me with equal joy.

"Welcome to Make-A-Friend! Will you be

making a friend today?"

The employee looks around as if to make sure we don't have a child with us, but I nod enthusiastically, nonetheless.

"Oh yes. And I'm very excited to do so."

I don't get to talk to many people, and I suddenly become hyper aware of my words. I squeeze Anne's hand for comfort and when she squeezes back it gives me the strength to continue on.

"I know exactly which one I'd like. Please."

"Well let's begin then. Which friend will you be taking home today?" the smiling woman asks as she leads us to an area with dolls and unfilled polyester animal pelts in boxes below them.

I make a beeline to the bright orange display animal that caught my attention from outside, taking the matching empty pelt from the bin underneath it.

"This one. This one is perfect."

Anne's eyebrows raise as she lets out a loud giggle. "That is perfect for you, Ori."

"Let's continue," the woman says, leading the way to a large, brightly colored machine.

In front of the machine are little things shaped like brains. I look at them curiously, wondering whatever they could be for.

"Would you like to add a memory for your friend?" the woman asks.

"No," Anne replies at the same time I reply, "Yes."

When I look at her questioningly, she says "They cost extra."

"My friend needs a memory, Anne," I insist.

With a sigh she nods to the employee. "Alright. Memory it is. I can't say no to that face."

"Now, what I need you to do," the employee begins, "is hold this mind carefully in your hands and make a wish."

I take the mind and gently cup it in my palms. With my eyes closed I think of the most important thing I could ever think of.

I wish Anne and Carl would live forever and be the happiest people ever.

I open my eyes and tell the employee "All done," before it occurs to me—I referred to Carl as a person. Ah well, I refer to myself as a man, and I'm a pillow.

"Next, I want you to give the mind a good pinch until you hear a click. When you do, say a very quick message. When you're done, click it again. From that point on, whenever you click the button, you'll hear the message you recorded."

I wrack my brain for the perfect thing to say but there's only one thing I'd ever want to repeat over and over forever, one thing I know I'll always mean.

Click. "I love you, Anne." I click the button again, then hand it to the employee.

"Wonderful." She puts the mind inside the head of the orange pelt, and we walk to the large machine. "Now, I'm going to place this on this tube right here and you're going to press this big, blue button. That's going to fill your friend all up with stuffing. Are you ready?"

"Absolutely!" I declare.

Anne smiles at my excitement, her initial grumpiness finally worn off.

"You're so cute, Ori."

"And don't I know it," I say with a wink that makes her giggle.

The employee places the item on the end of a tube. After a countdown, I press the blue button.

A happy jingle plays as the stuffing fills the pelt, turning it from flat, orange, fur, to my new stuffed friend. She tugs the filled animal off the tube and smiles.

"Now we just need to sew your friend up. It will only take a moment. While I'm doing that, please head up to the register and fill out its birth certificate."

As she walks away Anne and I grin at one another and clasp hands once again. I choose the name Luffy for the stuffed animal after a character in a show Anne likes. She finds it quite amusing.

At the counter Anne pays an admittedly preposterous amount for my new friend. She fills out the birth certificate, as I unfortunately can't write yet—type, yes. Watching Anne use the internet for years taught me to read, so I learned to type in no time at all. Writing with pen and paper is still a challenge.

When we get my new stuffed animal and leave the shop, Anne stops me outside and turns to me.

"Ori, what made you want a stuffed goldfish so badly anyway?"

"It reminded me of you and Carl. You because I wouldn't have been brought to life without you. And Carl is my only friend. I know it might seem silly to be a grown man with a stuffed animal but...I think I needed that entire experience."

"I guess I understand the first part, but I'm not really sure I understand the last part."

"That's alright. I don't think a human could. No one but me could, actually. It's a bit lonely, being the only one who's like this sometimes. But I wouldn't trade it for anything. Just please know I love you very much."

"Oh, Ori." Her hand softly caresses my jaw as she slips a gentle kiss upon my lips. "Never change."

"Never."

CHAPTER SIX
Anne

We wander around a bit more, stopping at a bed and bath store where Ori scoffs at the "inferior pillows" before ending up at a store known for their novelty items and adult goods. There are a lot of tasteless or silly things here—a t-shirt that says, "Boobies for Bros," pipes for smoking less than legal substances, and edible panties. It reminds me of being a teenager. I only go in there to show Ori how weird we all were when we were kids who thought we were so cool. I didn't expect to find anything he liked.

Of course, being the strange being he is, he finds things he likes. At first, he finds a lava lamp and is absolutely mesmerized. Bright blue blobs float up and down in the light while Ori stares wide-eyed.

"We need one, Anne," he says.

"We do not need one, Ori," I reply. If I wasn't kind of broke, I'd be up for buying him whatever he wanted, but work is cutting back hours lately. "Just wait until December at least. Maybe it can be a gift."

He turns to me and smiles with his perfectly white teeth, and I already know he's going to say something adorably sweet before he does. "You're the only gift I need Anne."

But then his eyes flit up to something on a shelf behind me, and his head tilts. He walks past me with a determined expression. I can't help but be very curious as to what would make him stop so suddenly. When I turn around and see what he's looking at, I slap my hand over my eyes. *Please don't let him make a scene.*

"Anne," he begins at what I rationally know is a perfectly normal volume but feels like yelling in my head. "Have you ever tried one of these gadgets? Anne? You're covering your eyes. It's called a vibrator. This one appears to have some sort of suction bit on the outside. Would you like that? Anne? Why are you so red?"

Oh god. Kill me now.

"Oh, you're afraid someone will hear, aren't you. No need to be shy. I want the whole world to know that you're mine. But I suppose if you're not comfortable with the world knowing I'm yours then that's alright."

I uncover my eyes and see that he looks like a kicked puppy. "That's not what that means! I just don't like anyone hearing about my...preferences.

Except you, of course. Let's get out of here."

I take Ori by the hand and as we're almost out the door he turns to me. "Are you sure you didn't want the t-shirt that said *World's Horniest Dad*?"

"I'm extremely positive," I can barely say as I laugh. Ori joins me in my laughter and we begin our walk back toward the exit.

"I think this was a good excursion, darling. We really should go out into the world more often," he suggests as he wraps his lean arm around my shoulder.

"I agree. It was a lot of fun spending time with you, and I was only afraid a few times. I can really see this sort of thing being beneficial to my therapy, not to mention just being good for life for the both of us in general."

"There's only one other place we need to stop."

"The cinnamon roll place, I almost forgot. Thanks for reminding me!"

Ori guides me toward a dim hallway that says, "Employees Only" and I look at him, puzzled. "Two places then."

"Uh…this isn't a place for shoppers, honey."

"I know. I checked the mall map online several times before we came to prepare myself for our visit and noticed an odd area that didn't seem to be used for much of anything. All of the storage areas behind shops are used, obviously, and there are general mall use ones for cleaning, storage, security, but this one didn't appear to have a purpose."

We pause in front of an unmarked door. Ori jiggles the handle and finds it locked. "No matter," he says with a mischievous grin before turning one finger into a long point and shoving it into the lock.

After a second there's a click and the door pops open. After flipping the switch, it's clear that this room is meant to be storage for one of the few empty shops in the mall. Though this mall is fairly popular, the age of online shopping means a few empty storefronts here and there.

"Perfect," he whispers as he closes the door behind us.

"Ori, this is an empty room," I say with a raised eyebrow.

"Not quite. Have a seat."

He guides me to a stack of boxes on the floor where he immediately leans in for a kiss. I hesitate for only a second before meeting that kiss; he's impossible to resist even in these strange circumstances. His satin tongue glides against mine and I moan at the perfection. It's an almost painful sense of loss when he pulls away.

"I'm going to remove your pants now. Don't argue. I know you'll try to."

He's right, I would have tried to, but when he gets frisky and controlling, I can't help but comply. He tugs off everything below my waist and kneels down, spreading my legs before him.

"Fantastic. I imagine I'll never tire of this sight," he rasps out.

I run a hand through his silky, black hair and brace the other on the cardboard behind me. Ori pounces on me suddenly, face planted between my thighs, filthy, wet sounds filling the empty room.

"Oh, yes," I moan as I raise my hips to press against him. "Thank you."

It doesn't take long for him to bring me to a climax. Bringing me pleasure is Ori's favorite activity, and he's an absolute expert. He pulls himself away and offers me a cocky look. The man knows he's done well. His elegant fingers slip up and down through my wet slit as he gives me my next command.

"Now bend over, my love. We're going to

make this rough and fast. We can't have the security catching us, can we?"

I gulp and shake my head. "Nope, can't have that."

I turn around and bend over the boxes, ass in the air, waiting for Ori to give me what is sure to be a good time.

"Oh yes," he growls out. "Fast and rough it is."

CHAPTER SEVEN
Ori

My darling Anne presents herself to me like an offering, a sacrifice, a gift I may use to take my pleasure. When she's like this I feel raw, animalistic. I need to take her *hard*.

"Oh, Anne. How wonderfully I've been made for you." I slide slowly at first into her wet center, letting her adjust to me until I'm fitted inside her like a glove.

She whimpers when I push my hips forward, pressing against her deepest parts in a way I know is sensitive but a pain she enjoys. As a pillow I wouldn't have guessed pain was a thing that could be enjoyed and even now I don't like it myself, but Anne...a little bit here and there has proven to be pleasurable for her.

"Are you going to be good for me, Anne? Can you handle what I give you? Can you take *more*?"

She knows I will push her limits sometimes but I'll always, always stop if she seems to not enjoy something. We've had the conversations many times and now we can trust one another.

My cock grows inside her, stretching her wide. She whines and writhes against me as I rock in and out, gradually increasing my pace.

"Yes," she barely forces out as I grow even thicker and pulse in opposite rhythm to her heartbeat for extra sensation.

I take a clump of her hair in my hands and pull her closer. Leaning over her.

"You're a very good girl. You deserve a treat."

From the area below my cock, I branch out a tentacle but this one is a little different. I model this one after a flower-shaped device I saw in the novelty store and add a sucking bit that fits perfectly around Anne's adorable bud of a clit. When it latches on and begins to suck, writhing in quick circles against her as it does, she shouts out nonsense words and begins to tense up immediately.

"A treat for my sweet," I laugh as I hold onto her hips, thrusting hard and fast, taking my pleasure from her glorious cunt while I offer it equally to her sweet clit.

She cums before I do, tightening hard around me with a shout of my name. The hard squeeze of her sends me over the edge and at the last second, I pull out, feathers flying out of my cock and over her back, her ass, and in the air.

I brush the down off of her as best as I can and hold her to me as we stand together.

"I love you." I tell her with every bit of truth inside me.

"I love you too, Ori. Now I need my pants and we need to get out of here before we get arrested."

She gets dressed and, giggling together, we exit the storage room.

Only problem is, we run into two angry security guards.

"Step back into the room, please," the shorter, bald one with the big mustache commands.

"Oh, we were on our way out actually," I say in a faux cheerful voice.

"Don't fuck around. It's listen to us or we call the cops. Your choice."

"Okay. We're listening," Anne says shakily, taking my hand and tugging me backward with her.

The security guards follow us into the room and the second one locks the door behind him. *Oh dear. That's not a good sign.*

"What were you two doing in here, huh?" asks the short one with the gray buzzcut.

"Just exploring," Anne replies.

"Yeah right," says the short one with a scoff. "We know what people do here. Now, what we want is a little show. That's all. Just take off your clothes and show us all the good things you did while you were alone. When you're done, you can go free. Easy as pie." Spit flies out from his mouth with every letter s, barely missing us.

"No," I growl. "No one forces my Anne to do anything she doesn't want to."

"Oh, it's Anne then? Well, hey Anne. Maybe if your boyfriend doesn't want to put on a show you can put it on with us? Would you like that better?" The bald, wrinkly guy laughs as he strokes her cheek with one tobacco-stained finger.

> *They threatened her.*
> *They propositioned her.*
> *They sexually harassed her.*
> *He **touched** her.*

Any bit of calm I have is gone, replaced entirely by the need to protect Anne. She is *mine* and she is mine to protect. I feel something surge inside me I've never felt before. Flashes of every time Anne has come home crying. Of Todd trying to harm her in her home. Men touching her at the

41

bus stop. A goose being taken to slaughter.

"Don't touch her," I spit out. "Never again."

My arm snaps out, my hand wrapping around the throat of the bald man. My eyes widen and the corners of my lips curl in a feral grin as his thick, brown mustache turns gray.

But I don't stop there. I keep draining him. When his skin turns thin, and his eyes grow sunken I don't stop. When his heart stops, I continue to *take* from every cell, every bacterium in and on him. I take everything until there's nothing but dust at my feet and a bit of hair in the shape of a mustache.

The man with the buzzcut pulls something off of his belt as I finish sucking the life from that piece of rubbish. He points the object at my chest and presses on it. Wires fly out of the little gun-like contraption and latch onto my chest. For a moment there is an expression of victory on the man's greasy face, as if something should be happening to me. But nothing does.

I pull the hook-ended wires from my body. A few feathers fly out in a puff from the tears, but they're quickly repaired, as I'm filled to the brim with energy at the moment.

I'm contemplating how to burn some off so that I can take him down without gaining too much flesh, when he snatches Anne and holds her in his arms. Rage blinds me and I move without further thought.

"You fucking fool," I roar as I graze his hand with mine. That's all it takes for him to still and for me to get a stronger hold on him.

His life force is draining quickly as I look to Anne and tell her, "Get away. I've got this."

Anne runs off somewhere. I'm laughing as I fill with more power than I can handle, feeling overstuffed, nearly overwhelmed but also so strong. Then the loudest noise I've ever heard rings out and a burning goes through my chest. I drop the man, he's nearly empty anyway, and raise my hands to the inflamed area.

There is a hole. Through my chest. When I turn my eyes to the man, I see him holding a gun. *Oh, that won't do.* I seal the hole in myself within seconds. Somehow even in his frail state he shoots again but once again, I seal the wound. I shoot out a tentacle and grab the gun, ripping it away. Finally, I take hold of his throat and look into his eyes. I say nothing as I watch the life force drain from him until he's nothing but dust.

When I drop him, I'm panting. I bend over, feeling a pain in my side. *Pain. That's odd.* I straighten up and look around to find Anne.

"Darling? It's alright. You can come out

now," I shout.

Anne peeks out from around some crates at the back of the room before running toward me and embracing me. She sobs as I run my hands over her smooth hair.

"Your glasses are all foggy, dear. Let me wipe them clean for you." I tell her gently. She hates when they get dirty.

When she hands me her glasses, I go to wipe them on my softest fabric but they only smudge. My brow furrows as I try a different area, but they only smudge worse. Confused, I hand them back to her.

"I must have gotten all dirty while fighting. Apologies."

"Thanks anyway, Ori. I've got it," she says with a sniffle as she rubs her glasses clean on the end of her shirt.

When she puts them on and looks into my face I smile at her, happy to see she's safe and sound after all of that trouble. She begins to smile back but her look changes to one of confusion, then one of fright as she screams.

"Anne! What's wrong?" I ask in a panic.

"Your face," she cries before backing away, covering her mouth with her hands, eyes wide.

"What's wrong? Am I flattened again?"

She shakes her head quickly from side to side. "No. You're...you..."

"Anne, what is it? Please," I beg.

"You're made of flesh."

CHAPTER EIGHT

Anne

Ori runs his hands along his cheeks, his nose, his neck.

"No. Oh no, no, no, I didn't mean to do this." Ori panics. He looks at me and clasps his hands together in front of himself. "Please don't leave me, Anne. I'll fix it somehow. Please."

I rear back in shock. "Leave you? Why would I leave you?"

"Because I have skin now. You won't want to touch me." A tear falls from his eye, and he wipes it away in frustration.

"Don't be silly. I love *you,* Ori, no matter what."

I wrap my arms around him, and he returns my embrace enthusiastically, holding me on the edge of too tightly before letting me go.

"We have to get out of here before someone comes in and sees us, darling."

"We're in deep trouble, aren't we?" I realize. "You...you *killed* those security guards."

"I don't think we will be. It's not as if there's a body. But it's better to not be caught at the scene of what I have to admit is a crime, and we're not supposed to be in this room anyway. So, come along. Our chariot awaits."

We take the bus. I barely register time passing as we do. Everything is just a fog until we get home and Ori walks me into the shower to clean up.

This time when Ori joins me in the shower, he doesn't get all messed up. He's totally fine, though he says he doesn't like the water as hot as I do. There is no romantic funny business, just cleaning off until my mind is clear, and I feel like I can function again. We both get out and wrap ourselves in the fluffiest towels I have and cuddle on the sofa.

"I don't have any clean clothes," Ori realizes. "Should have bought some at the mall I suppose."

"That Horny Dad t-shirt could have been yours."

We both laugh until I begin to cry, all my worry coming out at once. I'm so afraid for him and he barely seems worried at all.

"Aren't you scared, Ori? You've barely said anything?"

He sighs as he pets my hair. "Absolutely terrified. I don't know if I'll be able to return to myself or not. I'm so far gone. I don't want to be human. It's terrible. No offense."

"None taken," I reply as I stand and stretch. "I wouldn't want to be either. Personally, not a fan of humans, as you know."

A rumbling sound comes from below me and my eyebrows raise. Ori puts his arms over his stomach and looks at me with concern.

"My stomach hurts and is making all sorts of sounds. What's going on?"

"You're hungry. Let's go get you some food." I hold out my hand and he takes it, standing up to follow me.

"I don't like this one bit. Eating means I'll have to use the restroom. The *toilet,* Anne. I won't do it. Being *Human.* Disgusting. I can't do it."

"You'll be fine," I laugh. "I promise we'll figure this out together. Hey! You can finally try pizza! Maybe we can do pineapple."

"Anne, there are tiny hairs on my arms now and when you said that they all stood up."

As we walk past Carl's tank, I hear a ripping sound and feel the catch of my towel on the side of the table. My arms spin as I fall forward, then over correct and begin to fall backward toward the glass of the tank walls.

Before I can crash into it and cut myself to ribbons, Ori slides to my side, catching me in his strong arms. His hip, however, slams into the table, pushing it over just enough to upset the aquarium.

Carl's tank slides off the table, slamming into the floor with a mighty crash. The glass cracks then breaks apart, water flooding the living room floor. It goes flowing over our feet, as do shards of glass and aquarium rocks.

"Carl. Oh no. Carl!" Ori screams at the top of his lungs.

Ori sets me away from the glass then scrambles to his knees, glass cutting into them, and begins to frantically search the floor for his fishy friend. It takes him a moment to locate the goldfish. He finds it out of the water, flopping helplessly in the air.

"Carl, no, please," Ori pleads.

Tears stream down his face as he looks around for somewhere with deep enough water for Carl. There is nowhere.

"Carl. You're supposed to live forever. You're my only friend. I love you. Please." Ori stands and holds a still Carl to his bare chest as he closes his eyes and sniffles. "Why do I have too much life and you have none? It's not fair."

Ori's eyes snap open and he takes a sharp inhale. He takes another breath. Then another. I watch, confused, as he holds Carl in front of him and grins. Ori gets down on one knee, still holding the unmoving fish in his hands.

"Ori. Are you okay honey?" I carefully ask. I'm concerned he's having some kind of nervous breakdown.

"Oh, I'm wonderful. We're going to get our beta, my little omega."

"What are you talking about?" He's clearly having a breakdown. *Fuck.*

Then the fish starts shaking. Stretching. Pulsing. Growing.

What the fuck?

CHAPTER NINE

Ori

I can feel the life force draining out of me and the relief of it is one of the best things I've ever felt. When it leaves me, I can see Carl changing as it flows into him. I was afraid it wouldn't work but it is, *it is* working. Carl is becoming *more*. He's *alive*.

"Come on Carl. Just a touch more," I encourage him.

His body is having a difficult time accepting the amount of life I'm attempting to give it.. The little fish wants to *stay* a fish but that won't do any longer. If I want to stop having so much *flesh*, I have to get rid of a good lot of this human life force and Carl is the perfect receptacle since he needs to be revived. He needs to *live*. I won't let my only friend go. He's *mine.*

I push a little harder and finally it takes. I set him on the ground and step away until I meet Anne, wrapping an arm around her waist to watch Carl as he shifts into his new form.

"Ori, what's happening? Please give me a straight answer," Anne asks.

"Anne. Look at me."

She turns to look and when she does, she gasps. She raises her hand to stroke my woven face, my shoulders, my chest.

"You're fabric again. How?" she asks, wonder in her voice.

"I gave my humanity to Carl. Well, much of it. I still need to be part man after all. He'll be mostly man. Still a little bit aquatic though."

"He'll be what?" Anne gasps and turns her stunned gaze back to Carl.

"A little bit fish. I hope it's not too visible a bit. Though I suppose we could always take down another security guard and fix him if it was."

"Ori! That's not funny!"

"I'm only being practical." I notice a large change in Carl, and my excitement grows. "Oh look! He's growing so fast!"

Carl is changing much faster than I did. I'm so proud of him. He's already nearly Anne's size. He isn't in human form yet by any means. He's more the form of...an overfilled bag of trash. But it's something. And he's changing every second. Becoming *more*.

"This is so freaky."

"Please don't faint." I panic and grab hold of her, remembering what happened when she saw me mid-change. I don't want that to happen again.

"I think I've seen enough weird stuff to prevent the fainting now. But wow, this looks gross." Her nose scrunches up at the sight. I have to admit she's correct.

Carl's scales, gills, eyes, and fins swirl around in a mass of orange and white flesh. The throbbing blob only just forms into a shape almost describable as human.

"Give him a moment. I gave his form an excellent description of what to look like. Hopefully it works."

"You could tell him what to look like? What? What did you tell him to look like?"

I smirk. "You'll see."

We watch as the mass before us takes form slowly. Height much shorter than mine but taller than Anne, slender but with a fair amount of toned muscle, light golden skin with a healthier glow than I, as well as pale hair, ice blue eyes, and softly freckled cheeks. He also has a slight red-gold sheen all over his fit body, and he's most certainly *not* made of fabric.

Anne squints when Carl is finished

changing. The former goldfish stands still, panting and flexing his hands, staring off with a glazed expression.

"He's practically your opposite." Anne crouches to the floor, keeping her eyes on Carl the entire time. She stays silent for a moment longer before turning her head to me. "What now?"

"I suppose he's done, and I should help him. He's had an entirely different experience growing than I did. Honestly, I don't know what to expect. But here we go."

When I get to Carl he's still staring off into space, as if entirely unaware I'm there. With a shaking hand I brush back his flaxen hair and get close to his ear, before announcing my presence.

"Carl. It's me, Ori. Are you alright?"

Carl blinks slowly and turns his head to meet mine. His glazed gaze clears and focuses on my face as he sighs, his shoulders relaxing. A soft smile lifts his lips, crinkling the corners of his eyes before he speaks in a low voice.

"There you are, Ori."

"Here I am, Carl. How are you feeling?"

"Confused. What happened to me? How can you understand me? Wait, how do I know how to talk anyway? Where's Anne?"

"You know of Anne?" I shake my head. *Of course he knows Anne.* "She's here too, Carl. Let's all sit down and talk."

I lead Carl to the sofa where we sit next to each other. I toss a blanket over the both of us, as I haven't had time to make my clothes and we're both nude at this point; Anne is skittish about these things. Anne comes over then and sits next to me, burying her head against my side so that I'll toss my arm around her, which I do of course. I'd do anything my Anne wanted. Then I tell Carl his story.

"Carl, let me tell you how you came to be a man."

CHAPTER TEN

Anne

After explaining everything to Carl about how Ori brought him to life, and then having to backtrack and answer about a billion questions about Ori's origin, we all fall silent so Carl can take a moment to process things. There will be so many more questions coming up in the days—or even years—ahead from Carl. There's no need to rush things for the poor guy. I breathe in Ori's scent but don't find it; instead, I find he still smells like antibacterial soap. For the first time ever, I don't want something to smell like soap.

"Will I be able to stay here?" Carl asks quietly.

I sit up so fast I nearly smack Ori's jaw with my head. "What? Of course you can! You're part of our family."

With a smile, Carl blushes and lowers his head. "Thank you. I promise I'll be a useful part of this family. I'll learn all the things people do to find food and fight off predators and of course if you need a male for mating, I offer my services."

Air seems to stop running through my body

properly. I choke out a cough. At the same time, Ori barks out a laugh.

"You have many things to learn, Carl. We must discuss the concept of money. I'll take care of predators for the most part. As for the mating... we'll have to have a talk, man to man." Ori slaps a hand down onto Carl's shoulder, probably a little firmer than necessary.

"You're a good male, Ori. You saved my life and now you're helping me live it right." Carl smiles.

It's the biggest boy-next-door grin you could ever imagine. This guy really is the opposite of Ori.

"Now, let us prepare some food for the two of you. Thankfully, I was interrupted before I needed to partake in that particular ritual." Ori shudders, and I roll my eyes.

"Are we having pellets?" Carl asks. "Ooh, or those little brine shrimps? Or-"

"Carl," I interrupt, "people eat different things from fish."

"Oh. Yeah. Sorry." Carl ducks his head shyly and it makes me feel guilty for correcting him, even though it needed to happen.

"Oh Carl, no, don't be sorry," I soothe him, giving him a tight hug. He's so new to being human, there's no way he could be sick, so touching him doesn't bother me. "You're just learning. You'll catch on soon."

"Thanks, Anne. Okay, I'm ready to try anything."

Before we head to dinner, I grab Carl something to wear. He gets some gray sweatpants that are super baggy on me but barely loose on him, and a white t-shirt that says "Best Baby Girl" that my mom bought me, and I can't seem to get rid of even though I will never, ever wear it. I know it's ridiculous on him but it's the only thing that fits over his firm shoulders and biceps. The man isn't quite as tall as Ori but he's incredibly fit and solid...and I really shouldn't have given him gray sweatpants because I should *not* be looking at him the way I am.

We take him to the kitchen, and Ori and I decide just to make some salads. As a fish he ate the occasional vegetable. Salads are something he'd be used to, with the dressing and croutons and stuff being new things to try. Plus, I'm kind of stressed and don't really want anything heavy anyway.

Ori prepares the food while I get on my phone and hop onto a shopping website that is known for having fast delivery for its members. Some items can even be delivered overnight, so I look to see what affordable men's clothes can be sent as quickly as possible to fit Carl. I manage to find some cute, basic things for him and hit buy. He didn't really know what he liked, so it was basically me picking it out. I figure in time he'll develop his own style. For now, this will have to do.

Ori sets our plates down and takes a seat. "Anne, I believe I have an idea for a job. While I was putting together dinner, I remembered this part of a fanfic I read where-"

"Ori. I really don't want to talk about fan fiction now. It's been a long day. What we need is to eat dinner and go to bed."

"Alright, my love. It can wait. Anyway, given a choice, I'll always choose to be in bed with you."

CHAPTER ELEVEN

Carl

It was much easier swimming in the tank. I knew what to do and how to do it. Now I have to learn so many new things.

The salad before me has some recognizable things in it. Well, sort of recognizable anyway. Basically, they're green and leafy looking, and that's about it. I'll try the leaves first. I grab the fork in my hand and prepare to stab the leaf, but Anne reaches out her soft hand and places it over mine.

"Not like that. You don't hold the fork like you're going to stab it. It's more of a poke-scoop. Like this."

The warmth of her hand when it wraps around mine sends a shock through my body that heats me all the way through. I manage to pay attention to her lesson enough to catch on to how to use the fork properly, but most of my mind was occupied by the feeling of her skin on mine.

"Your skin feels really interesting," Anne comments. "It's textured almost like snakeskin."

"I was pondering that. I think it's the

remnants of scales," Ori guesses. "As if they've left an imprint on him."

"I think you're right," I say, running a finger along my own arm now.

It does feel different from Anne's skin. I hope she doesn't think I'm gross. I frown and get back to eating my dinner, trying not to let the talk of the difference in my body from theirs upset me. I poke-scoop the leaf several times before I finally get it right and bring it to my mouth for a bite. It tastes like I remember from nibbling it in the water, only this time there is a strange liquid drizzled on top of it that I'm not sure I like.

"What do you think?" Ori asks.

"It's great," I reply and take another bite.

I'm not going to criticize anything tonight. They could give me aquarium gravel and I'd gladly eat it. I eat the entire thing and manage to *mostly* enjoy it, as long as I discreetly wipe off the drizzled stuff. Anne is yawning by the time we're done, and I admit to feeling tuckered out as well. Ori cleaned all the broken glass and mopped the water while we ate.

"I hope it's ok that you have to sleep on the sofa, Carl. Ori and I already take up the bed."

"Well, this is the first time I'm really sleeping as a human, so I won't know the difference between a bed and a sofa anyway." I smile.

"Still. I want you to be comfortable."

"You may have the best pillow in the house to make up for it. The best pillow that's not me, of course," Ori offers, presenting me with a large, fluffy pillow. "Only the best for my best friend."

My heart warms at that. I've only been human a handful of hours and I've already got a best friend and a wonderful family. This is a scary transition, but I think I've got the best two people in the whole world to make it with.

"Thank you, Ori." I lunge forward and wrap my arms around him. He and Anne both laugh and hug me back. I'm so glad to have them.

When we're all tucked in for the night, I try to fall asleep but can't seem to, even though I'm very tired. My mind races with so many thoughts and questions. There are so many it's like I can't even focus on one thought at a time—until I hear Ori and Anne.

It's a sound I've heard before many times. Not to mention the fact that I've witnessed the actions that create those sounds in this very room before.

They're mating. Now there's *definitely* no way I'm going to fall asleep.

When I was a fish, I didn't really think much of it, obviously. It was just the two animals who kept me safe mating. I had a special fondness for those two animals due to them saving me from that scary place that mistreated us fish, but they were just big animals, nonetheless. I wasn't sexually attracted to them.

When I became human everything instantly changed. All my biological instincts are all mixed up now. I still feel like a goldfish in some ways, but in my loins...wow, everything is different. My mating drive now sees Anne as more than an animal. Much more.

Anne is the one who told the man in the shop he was an asshole for keeping me in that tiny bowl. Who held me in the plastic bag on the way home and assured me that I'd be in a real aquarium. Who spoke to me like I was someone that mattered, even when I was a fish. Her hair is so shiny. And she smells *amazing*.

My hormones are going wild. And also, it feels weird to say, but what my eyes are attracted to is different now. I see her large breasts bouncing underneath her t-shirt and her thick rump flexing under her cotton pants and I feel a rush to my groin that makes me grit my teeth. I would never have found those things beautiful before but now they're so attractive I *ache*.

Hearing them mating is bringing back all the times I saw them mate out here in the living room but wasn't fazed by it. I'm seeing those memories with these new eyes now and...*fuck*. I shift so that I'm lying on my back and when I look forward, I notice there is a tented area in my blanket. After a moment of confusion, I realize it's...my cock. I've never had a cock before so it's no wonder I was confused. This whole human mating thing is confusing.

I slip my hand under the blanket, softly gliding my hand along my stiffened member. Right then a particularly loud moan comes from Anne's room, making me flinch back. *That touch felt really good.* I sit still for a moment, wondering if I should do it again. When another loud moan comes from the other end of the apartment, I decide that yes, I would like to continue stroking it.

At first, I just try different types of touches, nervously stopping and starting, afraid of being caught. I'm not sure whether or not it would be frowned upon to do this but I have an instinct telling me it's meant to be private. Soon though I find a rhythm and way of squeezing I enjoy, memories of Anne bouncing on Ori's cock on this very couch running through my mind. I keep at it until I feel a strange but good build up along with a pull in the new balls I have. I move faster, my jaw tenses, my hips lift. A powerful feeling pulses through me, making me want to cry out with pleasure. I barely manage to stay silent.

If this feeling is why they are always mating, then *wow* do I understand it. I was already willing to help fertilize Anne's eggs if she needed it but now, I'm *very* eager to.

Ori had a brief talk with me earlier, when Anne was washing up for bed, and said that humans reproduce differently from fish, that they put their penis inside the other one's "vagina" to make babies. He didn't say where the eggs come into play but maybe that's different from person to person.

He did also say that sometimes humans do mating things with each other just for fun and not for reproduction too, so that's interesting. I *did* get the desire for Ori to chase me, and chasing is a mating behavior. Mating between two males obviously wouldn't create offspring, so I guess there is something to the "mating for fun" thing.

These thoughts are silly. Ori and Anne are my friends, and I shouldn't be worrying over this stuff. What I should be doing is resting so that I can be useful to the household tomorrow. I will do anything to be a good member of this family and if that means a good night's sleep then so be it. Now I just need to figure out how to make my eyes stay closed. *Sigh.*

CHAPTER TWELVE

Ori

"Carl. Wake up." Gently, I shake my friend by the shoulder. His pale blue eyes flutter open, flashing his boyish grin when he sees me standing above him.

"I did it, Ori. I fell asleep," he croaks out in a sleepy voice. "It wasn't easy, that's for sure."

"I'm proud of you. Now, cover up. Anne will be out of the shower soon and she doesn't need to see your erect prick staring at her." I point to said prick and watch as his cheeks turn red.

Rising in a panic, Carl hurriedly pulls the blankets back over himself. "Ah, I'm sorry. I'm not used to this."

After a brief moment of semi-awkward silence, Carl speaks again.

"So, for sleeping, I don't know. I miss the heaviness of water. I feel like if I'm going to relax, what I have covering me has to be something heavy. Something with pressure. Otherwise, it just feels…wrong."

"I have a weighted blanket I tried but wasn't

fond of that you can try out," Anne says from behind me, drying her hair on a towel. "And good morning by the way. Did Ori give you the clothes yet? Thankfully they were delivered early. Gotta thank the giant corporate overlords on occasions like this, I guess."

I have no idea what she's talking about when it comes to these powerful beings she refers to, but I pretend as if I do, regardless. I'll figure it out in time, I'm certain. I haven't taken the time to study politics but perhaps Carl and I can study them together and we can find out who our overlords are.

"He didn't, he just woke me up right before you came in," Carl says, hunched forward in his seated position on the couch.

"Oh okay, well let's have you try them on! I'm excited to see you all dressed up! They're not the coolest clothes ever but they're comfortable, I hope, and you'll blend in with a crowd."

"Blending in, *hmph*," I scoff as I brush the front of the black suit jacket I'm wearing. The suit is much simpler than the one I normally wear but it still looks fantastic on me.

"Yes, blending in. He already has golden skin with a scale pattern that we're going to have to worry about. And you made him very handsome, frankly, which will always draw looks.

We can't risk him standing out any other way. He's going to have to look like just a regular boy-next-door in his clothes," Anne replies.

The smile on Carl's face is so wide it nearly splits it in half. "You think I'm handsome?"

Anne rolls her eyes and crosses her arms under her bosom. "I said what I said. You know Ori wouldn't make you ugly, it's just a fact. Now let's get you in your new clothes already!"

I locate the packages for Carl and show him how to open everything. He needs a little assistance dressing, as zippers and buttons are not things that come easily to someone only a day old. He has the intellect but not the practice. It will come with time.

"There you are." With a proud smile, I step back and watch as he zips his hooded sweatshirt by himself. "You've got it."

"Only took about ten tries," he replies with a bemused smile.

"And next time it will take fewer."

I wrap my arm around his shoulder and gaze at the closed door, on the other side of which waits my darling Anne.

"My love did a wonderful job of figuring out what would fit you. Isn't she amazing?"

"She's really great, yeah. You've already asked me that a bunch of times, you know that, right?"

I turn my head and grin at him. "Oh, I know. I simply cannot resist any chance to show her off."

"Clearly," Carl replies with a laugh. With a quickness, he ducks out from under my arm and stands in front of me. He's fidgeting with his hands in front of himself, looking everywhere but at me when he says, "Would you chase me?"

My eyebrows pinch in confusion. "Would I what?"

Carl turns away and opens the door. "Never mind. It's stupid. Let's go show Anne the clothes."

The frown won't leave my face as he models his denim pants, white t-shirt, and black hooded sweatshirt for Anne. The sneakers she got him are even a perfect fit.

But I'm not pleased that he wouldn't open up to me about whatever it was he wanted to ask in the bedroom when he was changing. He asked me about *chasing* him. That seems rather odd. I wish he would have elaborated. I'm going to have to approach him about it. Not now when he's clearly not willing to talk, but in a moment when he seems relaxed. There should be no secrets between best friends.

CHAPTER THIRTEEN

Anne

I'm the worst person alive. I have the most amazing partner that has ever existed, who is perfect for me, who has like literally killed for me, and yet I'm thinking naughty thoughts about his best friend. What the fuck? Prison. I deserve prison.

"So, you're sure this looks alright?" Carl asks yet again. "You're not just saying that to be nice?"

"Believe me, I wouldn't say something just to be nice. You look really good. Great, actually. You're definitely pulling off the boy next-door vibe I was going for. As long as you keep the sweater and t-shirt pulled up to hide your shimmer when we're in public, you'll be fine. You don't have to hide it here though, don't worry. I think it's cool."

"You're not disgusted by it?" Carl's eyes open wide.

"What? Of course not! It's just a shimmery texture. Whoop-de-doo. Big deal." I shake my hands in front of me in an exaggerated motion. "Plus, it doesn't feel like human skin and, believe me, that's a huge bonus in this house."

Carl's face lights up with his signature wide grin and I can't help but match it. This guy is such a ray of sunshine, I'm so happy he's in our lives. He makes Ori so happy, and it will be nice for me to have someone else here who needs to do mortal body stuff to relate to and...his eyes are so pretty, his hair looks so soft, his lips look so full, he—

UGH STOP. Prison: I deserve it!

"Ah, I'm so happy, you don't even know. I hope everything I learn goes as smoothly as this."

"Me too! I want you to enjoy being human." We smile at one another for a moment before I pat the seat next to me on the sofa and wait until he sits down to speak.

"Are you having any troubles so far that you want to talk about? Anything we can do to make life better?"

He sighs and looks down at his fidgeting hands. "Well, there's the pressure thing. It feels so odd to move through the air. I can handle it throughout the day when I'm busy and not thinking about it, but it was hard to sleep when my mind wasn't occupied."

"We'll get you that weighted blanket right away, okay? Don't worry. And maybe we can see about getting you some time in the water to relax. Anything else?"

"I'm afraid to leave the house. Ori says we have to, that we can't stay locked up all the time, but I'm really nervous. I'm not that smart and I don't want to mess something up and get hurt or something." He runs his fingers through that feathery blonde hair, messing it up and leaving it in disarray.

"Why do you think you're not smart?" I'm surprised by that statement. The man was a fish less than a day ago and he's already sitting here having emotional conversations with me in perfect English. I wouldn't say he's lacking in intelligence.

"I don't know, I mean I can't read. I don't know anything about most of what you two talk about. Anything that I couldn't learn from just swimming around you two the last few months or wasn't transferred through Ori's life force thing isn't there." He drops his head into his hand and blows out a long breath.

"Oh, sweetie, it's okay. No one learns everything about the world in a day. Ori and I will both be here to help you and you'll catch on in like no time flat. There are things Ori still needs to learn you both can work on together. Shoot, there are things I'm sure I could learn too."

"You?" He lifts his head and turns to look at me. "I doubt you have to work very hard. You're super smart."

"Oh, thanks." I blush at the compliment.

"And talented. I saw all the beautiful drawings you'd bring home from work and even when I was still a fish, I could appreciate them."

"Really? That's so sweet of you to say, thank you." My blush gets deeper now. I can't help it; being noticed by a handsome man will do that to a girl.

"And you smell amazing. It makes me want to follow you everywhere. If I could be pressed up against you all day, breathing you in, feeling your warmth, I would be." His eyes are wild now, his breathing quick.

Well, now my face is just about on fire. "Oh. Well. I don't think that's really appropriate to say, Carl. That's very intimate and I'm only physically close with Ori."

A look of horror comes over Carl's sweet face and he covers his mouth with his hand. "I'm so sorry. I got carried away. I don't know how to control these…I don't know. I need to talk to Ori. I'm sorry, Anne."

Carl stands up and begins to march toward the bathroom.

"Carl, it's fine. I'm not upset."

"I just need to talk to Ori when I'm done in here," is all he says before he enters the bathroom and locks the door behind him.

Ori, I know, is in our bedroom using the computer to do something that has to do with getting a job. At dinner last night he began to tell me what his idea was, but I cut him off. I realize now I've been doing that a lot lately and that's really shitty of me. Just because I'm tired or in a bad mood or something doesn't mean I shouldn't respect his needs. He never complains and so I never know when I've upset him. I really don't deserve someone that sweet.

I don't want to go talk to Ori now when I know that Carl plans to, so I need to kill some time. Guess I'll just open those damn fan fiction sites and read more about the Omegaverse.

CHAPTER FOURTEEN

Carl

I'm so dumb.

The water splashing on my face helps to calm me a little. Water always does. Giving myself a moment to relax before talking to Ori will help, I think. I don't want to go in there all emotional.

Having all of these emotions is new to me anyway. I had some basic ones as a goldfish but none of these complicated ones. Navigating them is way too hard.

Alright. I dry my face off and head out of the bathroom. There's no sign of Anne so I go to the bedroom and find Ori sitting at the computer watching Anne's favorite anime, a look of deep concentration on his face and his phone in his hands.

"Hey Ori. Can I talk to you?"

His serious look turns to a smile at the sight of me, which warms me inside. "But of course. Have a seat."

Ori pats the bed beside him, and I sit down on it. I fidget a bit while thinking of exactly how to say what I need to without making him mad. Fidgeting seems to be something that has come naturally to me, I'm not really sure why other than having hands is still pretty weird.

"I think I'm having trouble with my hormones or something. I know we talked about mating a bit but it's just on my mind a lot. And I…I said something to Anne I maybe shouldn't have."

Ori's eyes snap to mine, a flame in them. Mine widen in fear briefly before his settle.

"You didn't threaten her, I know you know better," he says with a relieved sigh.

"Of course not! I would never! But I said something sort of sexual, I guess? Not crude but definitely more than friendly. It's because my hormones are going crazy, and I don't know how to control them." I tug on my hair in frustration.

Ori looks away in thought for a while before turning back to me. "I believe we need to take a walk. To relieve some stress. Anne and I take our Sunday walks to a quiet little park. You and I can go there alone, work off some energy, get you out of the house. Sound alright?"

I nod vigorously. "Whatever you think would work."

"Good. We'll go in the morning." Ori pats my knee and I sigh contentedly now that we have a plan. Then Ori speaks again. "And Carl. Whatever happens with Anne, remember this: she is *mine*."

My mouth goes dry as I nod my agreement. When I was still a fish, I saw what Ori did to that landlord and I wouldn't want that to be me, that's for sure.

"So, anyway," I desperately try to change the subject, "what are you doing?"

"Research. Sit and enjoy, it's an excellent program." He smiles at me, and I can't resist agreeing. There's something about Ori that makes it hard to say no.

CHAPTER FIFTEEN

Ori

It takes some convincing, but Anne agrees that Carl and I walking to the park while she's at work is a fine idea. She's so very worried for us and I understand why. Neither of us has ever been anywhere alone, and our social skills are lacking to say the least. But I'm confident. And there's something important that needs to be done today, between Carl and I alone.

Carl wonders at every sight along the way to the park. It's only a few blocks away, a straight walk, but to him it must seem like an incredible adventure. I would know how he feels. Only a few months ago I was in the same position.

"I haven't seen so many people since I was at the pet shop. And most of those people weren't very nice. They'd tap on my bowl and scare me. But these people just walk right past and don't do anything. Some even smile at us!"

"Something Anne isn't particularly fond of. She's had some unfortunate experiences with people so I can't entirely blame her for it." My darling Anne. So troubled and yet she carries on each day without having murdered anyone.

"I wish we could help her."

"Just being her friend does."

"Wow, look at all the leaves! Are they the kind we can eat? Is this where they come from?" Carl stops near a tree at the edge of the park and strokes a leaf on a low branch.

"No, no. Anne buys the groceries on her phone, and they get delivered to the house. The delivery people don't wear the same outfits as the overlord's servants, so I think they're just from a normal store."

"The overlords?" Carl tilts his head questioningly.

"Hmm, yes. I'm not well informed on them. I've decided we can learn about politics together. But for now, let's walk toward that wooded area farther into the park." I signal to a path that leads down into a forested area that's been kept wild at the edge of the city. This will be perfect for what I need to do.

"Okay! What are we doing down here? Wow, there's so many types of plants down here. We don't eat any of them? Oh! I think I saw a bird! Is it going to hurt us? Birds frighten me."

"You don't have to worry about birds, Carl."

On the path we pass by two young women. They're both clearly beautiful, though I have no interest in them. Anne is the only woman I'll ever have eyes for. Carl glances their way and I have a thought. When they are out of earshot, I ask Carl my question.

"Carl, how did your hormones react to those women?"

"Oh. Not really at all, actually. I mean, they were pretty, but I didn't feel anything."

"Did you feel any pull toward anyone on the walk here?"

"Nope. Must be too distracted or something I guess." He shrugs and keeps walking.

I watch the back of his head as he goes. He's so carefree, not aware he's being stalked by a predator. When he hits the end of the path, the beginning of the tree line, he stops and turns to me.

"Okay, what now?" he asks with a grin.

"Keep walking," I reply, no grin on my face.

"Into the trees? Isn't that dangerous?"

"I'll be with you."

"Oh. Okay." Carl nervously fidgets as he

begins to walk into the forest.

The day is bright and light streams through the branches above. The trees here are not thick enough to shut out the light entirely, only most of it. As Carl walks further in he looks back at me every few seconds as if making sure I'm still there. After we've gone in deep enough to not be heard by those on the path, I stop him.

"You asked me something yesterday and refused to elaborate when I asked you to repeat yourself. But I heard you, Carl. You want me to chase you."

Carl sucks in a surprised breath but before he can say anything I hold up a hand.

"Now I will."

I clasp my hands behind my back and take a few steps around him. Look him over to double check that he's in running shape. He is.

"I understand that this is something goldfish do when they are attempting to catch a mate. It is my hope that this will relieve some of your distress. As your alpha, it is my duty to ensure my pack is well satisfied."

There is a breath of silence in which Carl's face screws up in confusion, his head tilting to the side, before he haltingly asks, "Alpha? What are you talking about?"

A smirk lifts my lips and my eyes laser focus onto his. "It means swim, little fishy, as fast as you can. Go."

Carl's face blanches before he turns around, stumbling briefly over a tree root, and takes off in a run. It's a terribly awkward run; the man has barely had time to learn how to use legs, after all. But it's quick enough to make the game fun.

Laughing, I put my hands around my mouth to amplify my voice as I shout after him, "I'm almost ready to come after you. If I catch you, I'll nibble on your fins, beta."

Researching goldfish habits while everyone was asleep last night was quite enlightening. There are so many things we could get up to if he truly has retained many of his instincts. But for now, we run.

"Here I come!" And with that, I'm off.

I'm not the world's fastest runner, I'll admit it. I'm not *made* for it. But I'm determined—I have long legs, I've had more practice with them than Carl, and I won't run out of breath. I'll catch up with him in no time.

And I do. It doesn't take long to find Carl in a small clearing, hands on his knees, panting. His back is to me as I silently creep from between the trees toward him. He takes no notice of me at all before I pounce.

I take him down easily in his current position and though he struggles, he still ends up belly down on the ground. I lay my body flat on top of his and slam his hands on the ground above his head, pinning him in place. With a dark, low laugh I drop my head toward his neck and lean in.

"Okay Ori I got it now. You-" Carl begins, but I cut him off with a short snap of my teeth on his earlobe.

"Got you now. Nibble, nibble, little fish."

Carl groans as I nip his ear one more time, just barely, and grind my pelvis against his ass, pushing him hard into the ground.

"Ori, I get it. You're the dominant one. I know that. Okay?" Carl pants out. "But if you keep doing that I'm going to-"

I grind into him again, ensuring that he understands my strength, how easily I could take him down. My cock is hard and thick against him, and I make sure he feels how huge it is between us.

"Do you feel how strong I am, Carl? Even with what I'm made of?" I growl next to his ear.

"Yes, Ori," he replies, still panting.

"Do you feel the size of my cock? You could

never pleasure Anne the way I could. But you want her, don't you? You want to stick your cock into her perfect cunt. Taste her impeccable flavor. Don't you?" I free one of my hands, clasping both of his in one of mine. I tug his hair back with my loose hand so that I can see his eyes when he answers.

"Yes. I'm sorry. I want to mate with her. She smells so good, and I want to give her my milt and I bet she has a really lovely ass and…Ori please stop pushing me against the ground because it feels-"

Straddling his hips, I grind against him over and over, forcing his groin into the dirt. Unexpectedly, moans of pleasure are reluctantly wrenched from Carl as he finally stiffens and shudders underneath me.

Perhaps I've gone too far.

"Ori," he *whimpers*, "I…you know."

"Hmm. Well." How awkward. I clear my throat and sit up some. "You won't be touching Anne without my permission. You understand?"

"Yes, Ori. I'll wait for permission to touch her."

"That's not really what I meant but…you know, good enough. Let's go home."

CHAPTER SIXTEEN

Carl

I'm so confused.

Ori and I walked home after that, neither of us speaking at all most of the way. The fronts of my pants and sweatshirt were filthy, as were Ori's knees, and we got a few strange looks from passersby. Ori ignored them all, acting as if they didn't even exist, except once when he stopped a woman to ask where she had purchased her backpack.

The bag was decorated in soft pastel colors and featured characters from a classic anime that Anne loves. I guess he wants to buy one for her. The woman he spoke to stumbled over her words, blushing and unable to look him in the eye as she told him where to find it. Her behavior was strange, as prior to Ori speaking to her she had seemed quite reserved. When we were done talking to the woman and nearly home, I asked Ori about her change in demeanor.

"Why did that lady act so weird when she was talking to you?"

"She was attracted to me," he states matter-of-factly.

"How do you know that? You've already learned all the human social queues?" People seem really complicated, and I can't imagine ever being able to figure them out.

"No. I learned some from watching television for the years I was still Anne's pillow, you know. Now I learn things online when they confuse me. But in regard to that particular situation, the one you just witnessed, I've had personal experience more than once. Anne created me to look like a passably human anime character. It's a look that some find attractive and often they react the way that woman did around me. Anne had to point it out on one of our Sunday walks."

We reach the apartment building and head inside. *Am I attractive?* The thought appears in my mind as soon as we step through the threshold, and I can't get it out.

Ori walks into the bathroom, I hear the water turn on. I can smell the food Anne is cooking now that she's home from work. It's a scent I don't recognize, and I don't look forward to another night of eating something new. But eating with her, that I'll do.

Am I attractive?

Anne is beautiful, though she tries hard to

hide it. Ori is handsome and not afraid to flaunt it. But am I good looking? Anne said I was handsome but what if she was just saying that so I wouldn't feel bad?

Now I'm feeling a little panicked. My stomach hurts, my lips feel numb, and my heart is racing. *What if Anne and Ori think I'm hideous?* Sweat beads on my forehead and I feel like everything is too close—it's going to crash into me, crush me. *What if Ori never gives me permission to touch Anne?* I sink to the floor and curl up, feeling like I can't breathe. *What if they don't want me around at all?*

"Carl? Hey, what's going on?" I hear a voice that sounds like it's coming from far away even as the speaker's hand lands gently on my shoulder. "Carl, sweetie, can you talk to me? What happened?"

"What happened to my friend? I only stepped into the restroom to cleanse my hands and legs. Is he hurt?"

"I don't know, he won't say anything. He's just curled up and shaking. Hey, Carl, please say something."

It takes all my willpower, but with a shaky breath I manage to speak. "Please don't leave me."

Suddenly, a soft body is wrapped around

mine, holding me tightly despite my soil-covered clothing. I can smell Anne's intoxicating scent caressing me. My breathing and my heart rate slow; I feel instantly calmer.

"Why would we leave you? You're our best friend. Why would you even think we'd do that?" Anne says against my shoulder.

"Because I'm not beautiful like you. There's no room for me. You two are inseparable and you'll get tired of having the golden freak of a friend taking up what little space you have. I don't have anything to contribute, and I'm not even allowed to touch you without permission. By the way, I hope Ori sees that this touching isn't my fault."

"Noted." He replies haughtily.

"What the hell are you two talking about? Permission? I'm not an object you can lend out. You're both lucky I can stand your touches anyway." Anne spits out.

Lucky is right. No one on the planet is as lucky as I am to have these two.

"But whatever. That's not the point of this. What matters is that you know we won't ever stop caring about you, Carl. This is your home too now. And yeah, we'll probably need a bigger one but, on my paycheck, we can't afford much right now. We'll do our best to make things comfortable with what we have. And the attractive thing? Have you seen yourself? You're gorgeous. You look like you should be part of a fairytale, rescuing me from danger and taking me to your magical ocean kingdom."

Anne inhales deeply against my shoulder. It strikes me that she's inhaling my scent. I wonder what she'll find.

"You smell like the forest. Did something bad happen to you two there? Is that why you're acting this way?"

"No. It was fine. Ori and I talked. He told me I'm the beta and he's the alpha. I don't really know what that means but I think I got the point. Ori is in charge here."

Anne scoffs. "He thinks he's in charge."

"Anne," Ori speaks up. "I've been trying to speak to you about the Omegaverse."

"Is this really the time?" Anne says in frustration, gently releasing me from her hold then sitting up, tugging me along with her.

"I know the things I like are silly to you, Anne, but they've helped me get through days that would have been otherwise torturously dull. Yes, I may be still and patient but only because I have a lively imagination. Only because I've heard or seen or read fantastic things to feed into my well of creativity. I could sit as a pillow for years entertained by nothing but the memory of a few stories and my darling Anne. Now I only desire to share some of what's inside me. That's all. And in this case, I believe it could help."

Anne stands and wraps her arms around Ori. I tug my knees to my chest and set my chin on them, watching the two lovers embrace.

"Ori, I'm sorry I've been so dismissive and stubborn and, well, rude. I've taken my frustrations with work and bills and all that and let it mess up my head and it should not be affecting the way I treat you, ever. I love you. Tell me everything. I want to hear it. Carl too, right?" Anne turns to me and offers me a smile that I can't resist returning. *She didn't forget to include me.*

"Yeah, I want to hear too."

"Alright. First off, a warning. The plan includes Carl mating you."

CHAPTER SEVENTEEN

Anne

"What?" Carl chokes out. "I thought we weren't supposed to do that."

"Excuse me?" I ask, incredibly shocked.

"Yes. Alright so, the Omega-"

"Ori!" I interject. "What about Carl and me? What the hell?"

"I'm explaining. You said you'd listen. So here I go. The Omegaverse is a trope in fiction. There's a lot to it, I can provide some examples of stories if you'd like, but for our situation I'd like to simplify it. Keep it more specific to our situation."

I listen to him as patiently as I can without interrupting. Omegaverse is a pretty well-known trope among people who read the types of things I do, so I don't really need a primer. I just need to know why he's trying to *mate me* to Carl.

"Initially there were only the two of us, Anne would be the omega, which is the submissive member of the pack who generally gets bred by a strong mate, and I would be the alpha, the one in charge who generally does the breeding. We didn't have a beta and I thought that would be fine enough, as betas are complicated in Omegaverse lore, anyway."

Ori paces the hall with his hands clasped behind his back as he tells us his fucked-up plan. I contemplate whether or not he should have access to the internet.

"But then we were blessed with Carl. I created him physically to be someone I believed you would find attractive, Anne. A fairytale prince, a light to my darkness. Impossible for you to resist. As he was generated using my life force, there was no chance he wouldn't have at least *some* attraction to you in return. My entire being is dedicated to my love for you, Anne. Carl inherited some of that. As it turns out, Carl, being a young fish-man in his prime, is filled to the brim with mating hormones. He also has a specific desire for you, Anne, beyond what I gave him. He didn't glance once at any of the beautiful people we passed today, but whenever you're around he lights up like a match.

"Carl is also submissive to me. I proved it today, in fact. This is a necessary characteristic for our ideal beta. Today during our outing, I also found out that Carl does, in fact, ejaculate a kind of fluid. This is also beneficial as I do not. If we are roleplaying, we need someone to stuff you with cum."

"Ori!" I shriek.

I turn to look at Carl only to find him covering his face with his hands. It's then that I take in his dirty clothes and start to wonder what exactly happened in those woods and how Ori knows about Carl's jizz.

"Ori, you're talking about this like it's all real-life stuff, but you also know it's actually roleplaying. So, what is it? This all sounds insane." I fling my arms out in frustration, nearly smacking Carl. "Sorry, sweetie."

"Of course it's not real. But we're real. And we have real desires. I know you desire me; you've shown me nearly every day for months. And, Anne, I know you desire Carl."

"Ori, stop right now. You know I love you and I would never be unfaithful to you."

Ori grabs me in a big hug and snuggles his face into my hair before pulling away.

"Of course I know that. You're mine. Whatever develops between the two of you will be its own relationship, as will the one that develops between all three of us. Neither will change the one between you and me. That's ours."

I sit on the floor next to Carl again and lean my head on his shoulder, making sure he feels included too. This time Ori joins us on the floor, his long legs crossed in front of him.

"Carl. The world is brand new to you. You're flooded with hormones. You shouldn't be getting involved in a triad. I do like you, though. He's not wrong."

"I so rarely am," Ori whispers. I choose to ignore him.

"So eventually...I mean, honestly, I don't even know what this Omegaverse thing had to do really with this whole discussion when we could have just talked about it in a normal way. Why is he so weird?" I grumble.

Carl snickers. "You made him, you tell me."

"Oh no, I'm not taking responsibility for that. The personality was fully intact when I found him."

The both of us start laughing until we fall backwards, facing the ceiling, tears in the corners of our eyes. Ori just watches, shaking his head. When the two of us finally calm down I turn my head to Carl's only inches away from mine now.

"But really. It's too soon for you to be getting involved in an intimate relationship."

"You were intimate with Ori the first day you met him."

"That was different! Things were really weird. I was a different person then."

"What if we took things a little slow then? Because I know what I want, Anne. At this point it's you who needs to be comfortable. I'm fine." He smiles that fairytale smile, and I want to kiss him right there.

Glancing at Ori first to make sure it's okay, he nods. So, I do. I place a soft kiss on Carl's plush lips, pull back several inches, and wait.

Carl's pupils grow massive in his ice blue eyes. He blows out a long breath, staring at the ceiling. I wonder if I should give up on him but right then he sits up and places one golden hand on the back of my neck, drawing my mouth toward his.

This kiss is a little sloppy, the skill a little lacking, but it's fantastic, nonetheless. He's going to be an amazing kisser once he gets used to his body. I return his attempt at hormonally frantic kisses with gentle guidance, using show rather than tell to teach him how to use his mouth. He takes to it *very* quickly and soon I'm whimpering and pressing my chest against his.

I thought I wouldn't be able to touch someone made of flesh like this, but Carl is different. When I stroke his cheek, I can feel that wonderful texture like snakeskin, not human skin. He doesn't smell like a human, he barely smells like anything, and the scent he does give off is fresh and bright. And he tastes like water. Not like distilled water, but like spring water. Slightly tinged with minerals but clean and refreshing. Nothing about him makes me feel anxious or disgusted or afraid. He's wonderful.

After several moments of passionate kissing, Carl pulls away with what I can tell is some reluctance. "Anne. If we don't stop now, I won't be able to stop at all."

Realizing I feel the same way, I just nod my head against his cheek. We lay there, breathing one another in, a world of possible futures between us.

Too many futures. So many possibilities. So much could go wrong. I don't want to hurt this sweet man. This man who has never caused any harm to anyone. Why would I ever choose to hurt him?

And then the scent of earth finally hits me.

"Oh. Oh no. You need to change now, and I need a shower. *Ugh*." I stand up and scurry toward the shower, hands held to either side of me. There are bits of dirt stuck to the front of my clothes and I can't help but think that it's on my hands or in my mouth or eyes. It's going to make me sick; it's going to make Ori and Carl sick. I just know it. I need to wash *now*.

"Fuck fuck fuck," I chant as I run the water in the shower, making sure it's as hot as I can handle. I strip off my clothes, placing them into the plastic bag-lined hamper, and get under the steaming stream.

The near blistering heat begins to soothe my anxiety almost immediately. When I begin to scrub with my antibacterial soap, it's as if I can feel it physically run down the drain with the suds. They don't understand that I'm doing this to protect us. That we need to be clean. No one understands. I scrub harder.

CHAPTER EIGHTEEN

Carl

I find some clean clothes and head to the kitchen right away. My stomach had begun rumbling and there can be no discussing feelings while hungry. I'm pretty sure Anne is going to want to discuss some stuff when she gets out of the shower because she was acting pretty weird. So, food.

When I get to the kitchen, however, I realize I have no idea how to cook. Or what anything even is. It's overwhelming. After trying and failing to figure out what is inside some of the boxes in the cabinets, I sit at the table and lay my head in my arms in defeat.

"You hungry?" Anne asks from behind me.

I nod my head as I raise it. "Very hungry. I don't know how to find food yet. I'm sorry that I can't provide food for us. I'm a failure."

"A failure? You haven't even had a chance to try. How could you fail?" Ori asks from behind Anne.

"You knew how to do so much more stuff

than I do by the time you'd been around two days, Ori."

"Well, not really. I mean, I knew a lot of information and the general concepts behind things by watching Anne but *doing* them is an entirely different matter. Anne and I didn't do much more than lay around and have sex for several days after I was made, frankly." Ori takes a seat next to me and Anne sits next to him.

"Oh. If you learned so much stuff from watching Anne, how did I learn all this stuff? I know a lot that I don't remember learning at the pet shop or while I was here."

"You learned it through my life force, I suppose. I'm not entirely sure but I think so anyway. I have a feeling we're in territory that hasn't been well explored, so the answers may not be easy to come by. This is all new to me, too."

"To all of us," Anne says with a bemused expression.

"I didn't think about it that way. What should we do now?" I look back and forth between the two of them, hoping one of them has the answer, but the way they're looking at each other it doesn't appear that they do.

Finally, Anne clears her throat. "Maybe, we just…live. Like, you two really need to learn how to be people with full and joyful lives outside of the apartment. And I need to get back on track with getting over my fears. I had a panic attack again tonight like I haven't for a while, and I can't do that anymore. So, let's just be individuals. Learn. Grow. See what happens."

Everything is silent for a moment except the soft, dry sound of Anne's fingertips rubbing together underneath the table. Suddenly, Ori stands up so fast from the table his chair is knocked backward.

"Are you breaking up with me?" he asks in a panicked voice.

"Oh god no," Anne replies, grabbing his arm in comfort. "Never. Never, ever. I just think you should get a job and maybe a hobby. Wow. I really need to do a better job of explaining things."

"A job? Me too?" I ask as I watch the two of them snuggle together in Ori's relief.

"Yeah, you too. Though, of course we won't expect anything right away." Anne assures me. "But…well, this is harder to say, but I think there shouldn't be anything romantic going on between us. You really need to discover who you are as a person. If I could do things over with Ori, I would let him discover who he was too. It's too late for that now, obviously, but it's not too late for you, Carl."

I sit back in my chair in a slump. There's no point in arguing; a no is a no. But I *will* find a way to win her over.

A job and a hobby. I have no skills. I can't even read. What the heck am I going to do?

CHAPTER NINETEEN

Carl

Anne wanted to wait, so I waited. For months. Now I'm standing near someone else.

She has long, red hair that flows over the front of her perky breasts, which are barely covered by a yellow bikini top. Her skin is fair, freckled, and flawless. When she walks her hips sway from side to side and everyone has to stop and stare, it's so hypnotizing. She's smart as a whip, funny, and she swims faster than all the other girls. Her name is *Emma*, and everyone wants to mate with her.

"Heya Carl. Your shift almost over?" she asks in her adorably raspy voice, bouncing on her toes at my side.

"You know it is, Emma. You ask every day." I gently shove her on the shoulder in a playful way. She *does* ask me every day. And she asks the same follow up question too.

"Well, then, maybe would you like to go out after? With me, I mean." She twists her hands shyly in front of her in that sweet way that drives a certain type of man mad.

Giving another look around the pool to make sure everything is alright before shooting a quick glance at Emma, I shake my head and sigh. "No, thank you. I'm busy. And here's Josh, that's my cue to go."

Everyone wants to mate with her except for me, that is.

"Okay fine," Emma pouts as Josh comes up to me and takes over.

I've been working as a lifeguard at this indoor pool these last few weeks, which should turn into an outdoor job once the weather warms up. It took a little bit for me to get this job, but I think it's obviously pretty good for someone who was very recently a fish. Going through all the trouble to get set up with all the "legal" documents needed to apply was worth it.

First, Anne had to come up with fake identities for Ori and me, which is apparently not easy at this time in history when everything can be verified online. But she managed to do it with time and money and the help of this really sketchy guy. We all decided to take Anne's last name so now we're Carl, Ori, and Anne Athans.

Then I had to learn to read and write enough to pass the lifeguard classes and...boy, that was tough. I worked on it day and night though, and I actually took to it a lot faster than I thought I would. I think it was probably because of Ori's force-thing-whatever but Anne likes to say it's just because I'm smart. I'll let her think that if it makes her like me more.

Once I could fumble through the reading and writing I took the necessary classes. I passed those with flying colors. Turns out, I'm a really good student! Maybe someday I'll go to school for even more stuff. Ori wants to learn about politics and geography for some reason so maybe we can do that together.

Once I got through my training it wasn't too hard to find a job. I'm pretty likable apparently, and I can swim better than just about anyone. The only thing that was tough to deal with at first was my golden, shimmery skin. People were pretty curious. I would kind of clam up when they asked about it. Now I'm good at answering in a natural manner. I just say it was a cosmetic procedure I got done overseas, sort of a new kind of tattooing, and people believe it.

So yeah, I really like this job. It's nice when I actually get to be in the water and not just standing or sitting around especially. I miss Ori and Anne but I know they have their own things going on during the day anyway and I'll get to see them when my shift is over.

Today, the locker room is hot and grimy as usual. I make sure to keep my sandals on like Anne told me to when I'm in here because apparently there are creatures or something lurking on the floor waiting to stick to people's feet. Yuck. When I go to grab my bag out of my locker it gets stuck and, try as I might, I can't seem to get it out.

"Hey, let me help," a smooth, rich voice offers.

A pair of deep brown, muscular arms reach over me and easily pull my bag from the locker. Ahead of me is a set of glorious pecs, glistening with sweat from the heat of this steamy room. I raise my head and look into a pair of beautiful brown eyes, framed by curling black lashes.

"Thanks, James," I say. "I don't want to be late for my ride again."

James is a swimming instructor here and he's a really cool guy. Everyone likes him and I have lunch with him sometimes.

"No problem, Carl." James smiles a perfect model-bright grin as he nervously scratches behind his ear. "I just, uh, if you got one sec can I ask you something?"

"Sure! I managed to get rid of Emma fast today for once," I laugh with a roll of my eyes as we both chuckle.

"Yeah, so, I was wondering if maybe Emma isn't your type, you know..." He rubs the back of his neck and raises a brow with a knowing look I don't understand.

"Well, no. She's not. Which is part of the reason I keep turning her down, obviously."

"So maybe your type might be less of an Emma and more of an...Ernest? If you feel me?"

I scratch my head with my free hand and assess how James is acting. He seems a little different than usual. Then it hits me. He reminds me a little of that time Ori asked that lady about her backpack. *James is attracted to me.*

"James, you're very handsome. If my heart wasn't already spoken for, I would like to mate with you in several ways that could not possibly produce offspring. But I'm taken. I hope we can continue to be friends."

James blinks silently for several beats. He shakes his head a few times before huffing out one of his low laughs.

"That was a strange rejection speech, I'm not gonna lie, Carl, but I'll accept it. And yeah, of course we can be friends." He holds out his hand and I shake it like Ori taught me to do.

We say goodbye and I head outside into the

cold to catch my ride. Anne is outside in our car waiting for me in the parking lot when I get there. Now with three incomes, we're able to afford a car, and no one has to take the bus anymore—which is great because the bus sucks a lot. I understand that it's better for the environment, but when one of you is terrified of germs, and two of you are not human, the ride is kind of scary.

"Hi Anne!" I say as I hop into the front seat. "Where's Ori?"

He's usually with her when she comes to pick me up.

"Oh, he decided to do a special birthday show for one of his clients. She was paying extra, and you know he's been saving up to take us all on that mystery trip he's always talking about. He should be done by the time we get back home."

It turns out he's not done when we get home, I can tell because the red light outside of their closed bedroom door is on. After she takes a quick shower, Anne and I split some reheated veggie lo mein. I've gotten used to human food the last few months, I even like a bunch of stuff, though some things I still can't stand. I'll just never eat beef or maple syrup again and no one can make me.

As we're cleaning up our dishes, I see the color coming from the hall switch from red back to white.

"Hey Anne, Ori's done." We finish our cleaning and head to their room to see my best friend.

When Anne opens the door, I find Ori sitting in front of his computer monitor in the fancy chair they have set in front of a Victorian wallpaper style backdrop. Our new apartment is much bigger than our last one, and their bedroom is big enough to fit this small filming area for Ori's work. When he needs more room, he'll sometimes set up in the living room.

"Hi Ori! How was your day?" I ask as I sit on the end of their big, soft bed.

"It was fine. She paid quite a lot. We'll be taking that trip very soon." Ori grins charmingly, his hair slightly mussed, and his cheeks flushed. He must have just finished his assignment before we came in.

Ori zips his pants, buttons up his shirt, takes the time to straighten his clothing. I like to watch him put himself back together like this. He could, frankly, just snap himself into a new outfit entirely if he wanted to. After some experimenting, we've learned that his clothes seem to be shed in the way humans might shed hair or nails. When they're on him they grow from him like part of his body and when they're detached, they're inanimate. There's a lot to learn about the way Ori and I work but little by little we're figuring it out.

"Alright, all better. Now, how was your day, my love?" Ori asks Anne.

"Fine. I submitted the final designs for the characters. I'm really nervous but I think I've got this. Chandra is such a good supervisor; I really think she'll see the potential."

Anne started working at a new indie game company that is a lot more gender diverse and she seems way happier. Her health insurance covers much more in the way of mental health services and she's been doing really well in therapy. I'm so proud of her. The art she's been putting out lately has been fantastic and she's doing so much of it too now that she's not so anxious all the time. Ori and I picked out some fancy painting stuff for her Christmas gift and she's been doing a ton of awesome pieces. Our apartment is like a gallery. It's beautiful.

"If she doesn't see how wonderful you are then she's blind," Ori says before kissing the top of Anne's head. "Now, how was your day, Carl?"

"Me?" I perk up. "It was great, as usual. Except I had to turn down Emma *again,* and today James, of all people, tried to ask me out. That's so weird, isn't it? I never knew James thought of me that way. Mrs. Phillips also tried to offer me fifty dollars to give me a blowjob but I said no, obviously."

Anne makes a choking sound and nearly falls off her side of the bed. "Mrs. Phillips? Reverend Phillips's wife? She's like seventy years old!"

"Well, you're never too old to suck c-" Ori begins before Anne slaps her hands over his mouth.

"That's enough." Anne sighs before releasing Ori, who has a naughty smile on his face that tells me he will be showing Anne all about age and blowjobs later. "Anyway, why do you keep turning everyone down? I mean, Mrs. Philips I get, but Emma and James are great catches. Every day some absolute gem tries to bag you and you turn them down. Why?"

"I don't feel a connection." I shrug. "Unless I feel something, I'm not interested, so why would I waste their time pretending to be?"

"If you've never felt a connection, how would you know though? Maybe you just need to spend some time around them before it clicks or something." Anne insists.

"No," Ori softly interjects. "He's already felt a connection, Anne. Stop pretending you don't know it."

Ori places his hand over hers and gently rubs them together before intertwining their fingers. She looks into his eyes for several long seconds before letting out a long breath.

"I know," she whispers before laying her head on his shoulder and closing her eyes.

I get up and walk out, to go to my bedroom and be alone.

CHAPTER TWENTY

Ori

My Anne. My darling Anne. She's perfect in every way. Every way, that is, aside from her stubbornness.

"Anne, you're still rejecting him?"

I know why. She thinks I won't love her if she accepts both of us. And she worries for Carl, that he's too sweet, he needs someone of his own to be happy. She's wrong about it all.

"Leave it, Ori," she mumbles against my shoulder.

"Fine, for now. But only because I missed you." I turn and lift her face to mine.

"I was only gone for the workday," she laughs. "That's the same as always."

"It felt like forever. I could barely hold back during my shows due to thinking about you. I've been edging myself all day. It's been torture."

We've had to come up with special effects to replace the feathers. The people who watch my performances want to see me...finish...and I can't very well show them the real thing.

"Well, we'll have to do something about that then, won't we?" Anne smiles up at me with her eyes blinking sweetly behind her glasses.

"Yes we will. Undress for me, quickly. I can't stand waiting a moment longer, my darling. I want what is *mine*."

Growling the last word hungrily, I tear off my own clothes without care. I don't seem to need to worry about the energy to replace things anymore. Ever since I...well, *killed* those fucking pig security guards, I seem to have an endless well of energy.

Biting her lip, Anne removes her clothing, only pausing when she's down to her little blue cotton panties. I groan at the sight of them. She knows they're special to me, as they're the ones she wore the first time we were together. She lies back on the bed, heavy breasts waiting for my kisses, and spreads her legs, revealing a river of blue cotton between her thighs.

"Come on, Ori. Let's have fun."

"Oh, I believe we will."

Several hours later, after much fun was had, Anne is busy playing some visual novel while I'm on my phone using social media to watch hamsters run on wheels on a live feed. *Is this really what I need to be doing?* I scroll up to find a live feed of a strange old man dancing instead. *No thank you.* With a frown I toss the phone onto the mattress and lay back, stretching out.

"Anne, I'm bored. Come play with me," I whine.

When I reach out to rub her side I accidentally nudge her mouse hand. I hear a click followed by a groan. Anne's head flops backward and she spins toward me in her chair.

"You made me click the rude dialogue option on accident right before it auto saved. I hate clicking the rude dialogue option. Now he's going to hate me," she grouses.

"It's a cartoon. It can't hate you. Perhaps it will be fun to see what will happen when you aren't always nice to the characters for once. Besides, you should take a break, you've been playing for ages, and I miss you."

"Ori, it's been like maybe twenty minutes max," Anne laughs as she crawls next to me.

"As I said, ages. You need some sleep, don't you darling? You have to work in the morning."

"*Argh* when did you become the responsible one? Fine. Let me use the restroom and I'll be right back."

Anne gives me a kiss on the cotton cheek and yawns before leaving the room. My darling Anne. How I do love to watch her backside jiggle and flex and she walks away. I will never tire of it. My goal, though she doesn't know it, is to find a way to get her and Carl to live forever. I'll succeed, I know it. If I turned from a pillow to a man, I could do anything.

But that's a problem for later. For now, I need Anne and Carl to finally get frisky. They don't understand. Their joining needs to happen.

When I made Carl, he was made from *my* life force. That means he inherited the thing that made me who I am. And that thing is my love for Anne. That means he will, naturally, have love for her. As he is my best friend, I will not let him suffer without her.

And I know he's perfect for her. I made him that way. He's everything I'm not. Where I'm dark he's light. Where I'm selfish, he's generous. Where I would hurt, he would heal. She *needs* him and I will *always* give Anne what she needs. She is *mine* and I won't let what is mine have anything less than everything.

Besides, an alpha needs a beta, doesn't he?

CHAPTER TWENTY-ONE

Anne

Ori's right, I really do need to go to bed. My new job is so great, but it does start early. It's a lot more demanding than my last one but it's also much more fulfilling. Going home each day I really feel satisfied with the work I've done, and I feel appreciated by my coworkers and superiors. Getting up a little earlier or occasionally staying a little late is no big deal.

The bathroom light is on, but the door is halfway open so I'm guessing whoever used it last just forgot to turn the light off. When I open the door all the way, I see that I've guessed wrong.

We have a pretty big bathtub in our new place. It's something Carl really wanted because he likes to take long baths. And that's what he's doing right now. This time he's fallen asleep in the water. I always warn him not to do that because I'm super paranoid he'll drown or something, but he just laughs and tells me not to worry. I can't help worrying—that's like a huge part of who I am. But I have to admit he looks super peaceful right now.

I've seen him naked before when he was transformed, but things were more than chaotic and strange at the time so I couldn't really process it. Looking at him now, I see that Ori made him *very* well. I've figured out by now that Ori tried to go for a soft, fairytale sweetheart-type and he succeeded. Yes, Carl is covered in those golden almost-scales, but underneath is a strong body, perfect for rescuing damsels in distress. That soft, innocent face, with this built body, and a big... well, he's got a great combination going on. Really, really great.

I shouldn't be staring like this but I'm having a hard time tearing my eyes away. He's so beautiful in the water. My eyes drag over every part of him, stopping specifically to wonder at the strength of his legs. He's taken up running as a hobby. Mixed with swimming as his other pleasure, his body is...wow. When I bring my eyes back to his face, I see his eyes are open, watching me watching him.

"Oh! I'm so sorry. The door was open and I didn't realize you were in here." I stumble over my words, trying to explain myself as quickly as possible.

Carl smiles and sits, all those perfect muscles flexing as he does. "It's my fault. I thought I closed it. Sorry. I'll be out in a minute so you can use the bathroom. I just drifted off. Don't kill me."

He raises his hands in a defensive posture,

and I can't help but laugh at him.

"I won't this time, but you're on thin ice, buddy."

"I'll be sure to watch myself," he nods. Then he raises an eyebrow as he looks me up and down. "Though, I think you've watched me enough for both of us."

"Oh my god," I squeak out before rushing out of the bathroom back into my bedroom.

Ori is laying on his back, nude, molding his cock into a pitchfork shape. When I give him a shocked look, he shrugs.

"I'm only testing something. I think you'll like it." He snaps back into shape and tosses the blanket over himself, patting the spot on the bed next to him. "Get your pajamas on now and come to bed."

"Oh, I still have to use the restroom. Carl was in the bath. But I suppose I can get dressed and then go."

"Hmm. You walked in on him?" Ori raises an eyebrow.

"Don't start," I warn as I take off my shirt and begin the search for pajamas.

"Was he simply lying in the water? Was he

touching himself?" Ori asks with a mischievous grin.

"Ori, stop being a brat."

"Was he stroking his cock in the water? Thinking about you? Did you watch him, Anne? Did he cum?"

I slip on a cotton nightgown with a picture of an orange cartoon cat wearing a cowboy hat on the front of it. Ori does not deserve my sexy satin numbers tonight.

"No. Not that it was any of your business. He was just bathing."

I bite the side of my thumbnail to keep from rubbing my fingers together. This conversation is making me anxious. The truth is the idea of walking in on Carl and seeing him doing something like that is flooding me between the legs, and Ori messing with me about it is stressful. I know he wants Carl and I to be together, but I don't want to hurt Carl. He's so sweet and innocent. Ori and I are so close, and we will *never* part. Introducing someone else into that dynamic is a big fucking deal, and I'm worried that Ori is treating it like a game. Or that Carl doesn't understand the stakes. Because when it comes down to it, I'll never leave Ori and if I really care about Carl, I won't put him into a relationship where he could be pushed out by Ori. I know how territorial Ori is and if one day Ori decides he's tired of Carl, what then? *Ugh.*

"Anne," Ori says much more softly, seriously. "I shouldn't have made fun."

"No, you shouldn't have. You know this is a sore subject. But thank you for recognizing that." I crawl into bed next to him and lay my head in the crook of his shoulder.

"Give him a chance, Anne."

"Goodnight, Ori."

CHAPTER TWENTY-TWO

Carl

After work I go outside and see Anne isn't there, so I check my phone and find she sent a message. She says she has to work late, so I need to take the bus. *Bleh*. I hate the bus.

It's cold, my hair is still wet, and I'm feeling a little crabby today so waiting for the bus just feels like it takes a lot longer than usual. Last night after I got out of the bath and went to my room, I couldn't stop thinking about Anne looking at me. I jacked off several times because I couldn't freaking sleep. She wouldn't get out of my head. Now I'm tired, I miss her, and I want to go home already.

Finally, the bus pulls up and I pay the fare. It's pretty empty thankfully, so I take a big seat in the back and relax. The next block over a lady gets on who looks like she maybe hasn't slept in a lot longer than me. Unfortunately, she sits right next to me, despite most of the other seats being empty.

"Hey cutie, where you going to?" she slurs out in a breath that smells like menthol and bacon. She leans so close to me that a greasy lock of her yellow blonde hair brushes against my cheek, making me flinch.

"Home," I reply curtly. Maybe if I keep it short, she'll get bored and go away.

"You want some company at home, sweetie?" Another brush of her bleached hair against my face makes me press back against the cold glass of the bus window.

Her calling me "sweetie" makes me angry. That's what Anne calls me. No one else can.

"No. I'm not your *sweetie*. Please leave me alone now." I don't like being mean, it makes my stomach hurt. I just have a feeling this lady isn't going to take nice for a no.

"I can be your sweetie. You're too cute to go home alone." She brushes my cheek with one long, blue, dirty fingernail and I nearly gag.

"I said no. And don't touch me. Go sit somewhere else." There. Clear as day. There's no way she can misinterpret that.

And she doesn't. She starts crying. *Fuck.*

"You guys are all the same. Won't give a girl a chance," she blubbers while green snot leaks down her face. "You think you're too good for me."

I look around for an escape route, but her big nylon duffel bag is blocking the aisle. I'll have to hop over it.

"It's not you, I, uh, I'm taken," I mumble as I stand.

"Yeah right," she suddenly screeches.

Okay, time to get the heck out of here.

"Fuck you, liar," she screams as she lifts a knee and trips me as I attempt to hop over her bag.

I manage to catch myself on the handlebars so that I don't smash my face into the floor, but I don't prevent myself from slamming my knees into the ground and my hip into the side of a bench. *Fuck that hurt.* When I pull myself up the woman shoves me so that my chest slams into the top of a bench. *Ouch.*

"Go home to your mama, asshole," she shouts as the bus pulls up to the next exit.

The woman gets off the bus and runs away as I plop myself into a seat. I think about whether or not to report the incident but decide against it. That woman clearly has some major problems to deal with and I just want to go home to my Anne and Ori. I'm hurting and I need their comfort more than anything.

A few stops later, I limp home to our apartment and find Ori in the kitchen making snacks for Anne and me. He looks so handsome in the early evening light—his dark hair falling over his brow, his grin that always looks like he is about to cause some trouble, his long, pale limbs that move so perfectly gracefully. He stops what he's doing and looks up at me when he hears me enter the room.

"Hello there, my friend. I've got a little treat for you before dinner, coming right up." He raises the platter to show me the charcuterie board he's working on. A look of concern crosses his face as he notices my expression. He sets down the tray. "What happened?"

"I got attacked by some crazy woman on the bus. Not hurt bad or anything, more just made me feel sad is all. Stupid bus." I wash my hands at the kitchen sink and dry them on a paper towel while Ori looks me over with a frown. "It's not a huge deal, really. I'm just bummed out."

"Perhaps you need some water time, followed by a video game?" Ori smiles as he gently lays a hand on my shoulder.

I perk up at the game suggestion. We haven't gamed together as a household in a while, and it could be fun. I could use a silly time dropping banana peels and shells on Ori for a while. But first he's definitely right about needing some water time. That always makes me feel better.

"You're right, as usual," I lay my head on his

hand before I hear the front door open and close.

We both turn toward the sound. *Anne's home.* It's just instinct for both of us to go to her as soon as she enters. We always want to be where Anne is. But when we see her she holds up a hand and drops her purse and coat on the polished wood floor.

"Not now. Bad day. I've gotta get into the shower right away." She rushes past the both of us and into the bathroom, slamming the door behind her.

Ori and I look at each other with frowns on our faces. "There goes my water time," I grumble.

"Not necessarily. I'm sure if you explained what happened she'd be willing to share her time," Ori says, his smile growing wider and his eyes shimmering with mischief.

"Ori. You're going to get me into trouble."

"No. I'm going to get you the girl. Go. If it doesn't work then blame me, she can't stay mad at me long."

Well, he's right about that. "You think she'll be okay with it?"

"If you act pathetic enough, yes."

"Oh. Well. That sure sounds great," I

mumble.

With some hesitation I head toward the bathroom door. I can hear the shower running. My throat tightens up. *Is this okay?* With a racing heart and a determined set to my jaw I decide *fuck it* and turn the handle.

Today I get the girl.

CHAPTER TWENTY-THREE

Anne

Fuck, work sucked. I mean, I love work, it's just that we had a meeting about doing a joint project with my old company and I wasn't aware of it until like right beforehand. It was super awkward, and I nearly passed out from the anxiety. My boss was disappointed in my performance in the meeting but what the fuck was I supposed to do? My brain was in total panic mode the whole time. I just hope she doesn't hold it against me too much.

The water runs extra hot against my tense muscles, soothing them, and loosening the tightness that has built up throughout the day.

Then the curtain opens. Carl blinks at me with those impossibly blue eyes as I startle at his sudden appearance.

"Sorry for scaring you. I thought I could join you in the shower," he explains while his eyes are very much locked above my neck. "And maybe help you if you need it."

"I don't need any help to shower, Carl. And for the record it's rude to just open the curtain when someone's showering." His face falls and he looks as if he's going to turn away. But that's not what I want. I have to admit it to myself. So, I keep talking. "Why did you think to come in here today?"

"Honestly," he pauses and looks at me with a genuine look of sadness, "I've had a pretty bad day and could use some water time."

"Oh. Well. Of course you can join me then, I guess."

Okay, it's weird that we're showering together, right? But we're friends and we both need the shower so it's okay. Right?

"You want to talk about it, Carl?" I ask once he's in and we're both awkwardly positioned so that there's some water spraying both of us.

"Not really. I just want to enjoy this time."

"Okay."

We face each other and I stand there looking at the tiles because I don't know what else to do. Then he speaks and everything changes.

"Can I look at you?" Carl asks and his cheeks have turned red with nervousness.

My eyebrows shoot up in surprise. "You mean, like, my body?"

"Yeah. I've only seen you naked through the tank, as a fish. I'd like to see you as a human. I've never seen a woman naked as a human."

"Oh. Um. Wow. That's…sure." *Wow, that's a lot of responsibility.*

I stand with my arms at my sides, feeling more than a little awkward as his eyes graze up and down my body. They pause at my breasts and my pubic area longer than the rest of me, which is unsurprising. When I feel a soft tap at my navel, Carl steps backward. I realize his cock has hardened and decided to say hello.

"Sorry," he whispers.

"That's fine. To be expected," I whisper back.

"You're beautiful. I didn't know what to expect but this is better than whatever I could have imagined."

"Well, I'm the only woman you've ever seen naked when you've had human hormones. There are much better-looking ones out there. But I appreciate the compliment nonetheless."

"Don't put yourself down. Why would I care

what other people look like when what I have in front of me is already perfect? Already makes me feel like my heart is going to explode just from being near it?" His voice is starting to get louder, faster, and I can feel myself grow slippery between my legs. Not the wetness of water but the satin texture that comes with desire.

"You're so sweet. So incredibly sweet." I'm lost for words. Nothing I can think of can fit how I'm feeling right now for this man.

"I wonder how sweet you are. Ori says women enjoy being kissed between their legs. I've seen him do it to you before. Would you let me try? We've already kissed, would it be different?"

His eyes have gone half lidded and he steps closer to me, his hard cock pushing against my stomach in the most delightful way. Is this really happening? Am I letting this happen?

"It's definitely different. And what if you don't like it? I'm-" *I'm afraid you won't like me.*

"The chances of me not liking anything to do with you are zero. But if I don't like it, I promise I'll tell you. Okay?" He steps so close there is no more possible room between us. "We have to make this water a little less hot though, if possible, I feel like I'm going to boil."

"Oh," I laugh. "I suppose that's fine. Just for

you, sweetie."

CHAPTER TWENTY-FOUR

Carl

She's so beautiful.

I knew what she looked like but it was only in memories and those were my fish memories. It's like looking back through a slightly cloudy mirror. I can see it but not the details. Seeing her up close, in all her glory, is beyond words. I'll never forget this moment. And now she's going to let me touch her. *Taste her.* Has anyone ever been so lucky?

Well, Ori. But I'm not thinking about him right now.

Anne turns to lower the temperature of the water and as she bends over, I drop to my knees and pull her hips toward me. She yelps and tries to stand but I keep a firm grip on one hip and hold her back down with the other.

"Stay. I like this view. Can you spread your legs a little wider please?" I ask.

"Carl! This is not how you do it!" She protests.

"I've seen Ori do it this way. Actually, can you put one foot up on the side of the tub please?"

"I mean…okay." She does as I say, and I can't help but slide my hand up and down my stiff cock a few times when I see what's before me.

Now *this* I've never seen. They've always been too far away to catch this much detail. I've been missing out on something very, very, good.

"Are you going to just stare all day?" Anne asks with a nervous giggle.

I shake my head, realizing I've been staring at her perfect entrances for what must have been far too long. But how could I not? I can see *everything* like this. Her tiny asshole, those spread lips surrounding her treasures, the pink wetness I know is waiting hungrily for a cock to fill it, the little bud that Ori says is solely for pleasure. All of that and more is revealed before me, waiting for my mouth. *Fuck, I'm so lucky.*

"Oh, I'm going to do much more than stare. Hold on, pretty girl, tell me if I'm doing this right because you deserve nothing less than perfection. Okay?" I run my hands along the outside of her hips, her thighs, and I can feel her skin grow goosebumps.

"Okay," she says in a squeaky voice.

"Wow," slips reverently past my lips when I slide one finger through the slippery liquid along her entrance. I bring that finger to my lips and my eyes close as I delight in the taste of her.

I can see her legs shaking and I don't know if it's from strain or nerves or what, so I grab hold of her hips to make sure she's supported. Then, unable to resist any longer, I lick a long line up the center of the most beautiful woman in the world.

Anne moans and pushes back against my face, making me so happy. If she wants closer that must mean she liked what I did, so I do it again, but this time with more pressure so that she doesn't need to push against me. By the sounds she makes and the way the entrance to her cunt seems to clench up I think she enjoys that, so I keep going.

It seems she really, really likes when I focus on the clit area, so I make sure to pay that special attention. She cocks her hips to make it easier for me to access and soon I find myself directing my focus almost entirely on it.

When Anne starts making these really fantastic groaning noises, I decide to take one hand off her hip and slip a couple fingers inside of her to see what happens. It turns out that when I do that while gently sucking on her little bud she really, *really,* likes that. In fact, she likes it so much her legs start shaking and she starts shouting things.

"Oh fuck, yes Carl, yes," she's shouting as her insides begin to clamp around my fingers. "Just like that. Don't stop."

I certainly don't plan to stop, not when it's getting this sort of reaction. She clamps so hard around my fingers I can barely move them, and I can feel liquid inside her leaking all around. It's so silky and slippery, I imagine it all around my cock and moan against her clit.

"Okay, stop, it's too much, I can't take anymore," Anne pants.

I reluctantly pull away and help her into a sitting position, on my lap. I turn us around so that the water is splashing the back of my head and not her face.

"That was really fun," I say, realizing even as I say it how dumb it sounds.

Anne giggles and drops her head onto my chest. "Yeah, it was, wasn't it?"

We're both silent for a good minute at least, just enjoying the warmth and comfort of the water and each other's bodies. Soon, Anne lifts her head and places a hand on my cheek.

"Let's get out of here. I think we've got some things to talk about," she says before placing a gentle kiss on my lips.

I could stay in the water forever with her, but I nod anyway. I know we need to talk about this with Ori when things aren't all emotional. It's just...I'm not great with handling feelings yet and there have been a lot of them already. So many. Do people always have this many feelings?

CHAPTER TWENTY-FIVE

Anne

I want to throw up. I'm about to open the door to my bedroom and tell Ori what just happened. I rationally know he'll be okay with it; he's been trying to get it to happen for months, but I'm just like...*ugh.* So worried. What if he changed his mind all of a sudden? I can't lose him. I just can't. The knob is cold in my hand, and I wonder if I can somehow psychically freeze it in place so that I have an excuse not to turn it. Stranger things have happened to me, after all. But, alas, when I turn my wrist, the knob turns with it and the door opens.

"Hey honey. We've got to talk about something," I say right off the bat. When he turns to look at me with those bright eyes and that charming smile, however, I clam up.

"What is it, darling? Do you have some exciting news to share?" he asks with a knowing grin.

Ah. He already guessed somehow. I should have known. *Ugh.*

"I kissed her vagina in the shower and made

her have an orgasm," Carl states proudly.

"Carl! Oh my god!" I flop onto the bed and cover my face with a pillow.

"Well, to be exact, it wasn't just her vagina. It was her clitoris and her-"

"Carl, shut up!" I shout as I throw the pillow at him. He catches it easily with a smile.

"I'm just letting him know what happened so that there aren't any secrets between us."

"You could be slightly vaguer, I think that would be alright," I grumble.

"Oh, no, I don't mind the details at all. Please continue." Ori's smile widens as he sits all the way back in his chair, hands on his lap.

"Anyway," I interrupt with a clearing of my throat. "I thought we should let you know that Carl and I were intimate. I think, and I think Carl agrees– I hope or else I'm going to feel really stupid– that we would like to try whatever this three-way thing would be. I'm having a really hard time accepting it though because I don't want to lose you, Ori. And I don't want to lose Carl. He's become a necessary part of our lives. I don't want to destroy what we have just because Carl and I add romantic feelings into the mix. I'm all messed up in the head over this, you know? *Ugh*. Please tell me it will be okay, Ori?"

Ori stands up and crawls onto the bed to sit next to me, wrapping an arm around my waist. Carl hesitates for a second but after a look from Ori joins us on the bed on my other side, propping his head on my shoulder.

"It will be more than okay, my love. If it was anyone other than Carl, I would tear them to ribbons before turning them to dust for even attempting to court you. I'm sure you know that," Ori says before tickling my side and making me giggle.

"Yeah, I know that. You're pretty creepy sometimes," I chuckle.

"Creepy in love. But with Carl, no violence is necessary. I know he would never cause you harm and he would never do anything I didn't approve of. He's the best of men because he is, like me, not really a man."

I laugh at that. "And that's why I love you. No human stuff getting in the way."

"And probably the amazing sex as well." Ori shrugs.

"That certainly doesn't hurt." I kiss his cheek, and Carl buries the top of his head against my neck.

"I have an idea," Ori says as he leans back

on the bed, crossing his long legs in front of him. "Why don't you and Carl go on a date? Have a day out. Then we can meet back at home and spend time together as our little pack."

"Our little pack?" I ask suspiciously.

"Yes. What about it?"

"I'd like to go on a date," Carl speaks up, raising his head. "I think I even know where we could go."

I turn my attention away from Ori's clearly mischievous plans and focus on Carl.

"Oh yeah? What have you got in mind, sweetie?"

"Well when you drive us home you pointed out the cat café and said how you want to go there but can't because Ori and cats don't mix. We could go if it's just you and me," he smiles boyishly and I can't help but return the grin. He's such a ray of sunshine.

"That is such a great idea, Carl. I can't believe you remembered that!" I hug him and breathe in that light, clean scent he has.

"I remember everything about you, Anne. You're the most important thing in the world to me." Carl brushes the hair back from my brow and I can feel tears pricking the corners of my eyes.

How the hell did I get *two* incredible guys? I'm really ripping off some chick out there who has lost the guy lottery and now has no one. I swallow my feelings back and blink my eyes a few times before speaking.

"Cat café it is. Tomorrow morning. I'll drive."

CHAPTER TWENTY-SIX

Ori

The duo went to the café this morning and I've gone out to take care of some private business. I don't like keeping secrets from them, but I don't want to let them down if what I'm trying to do doesn't work out. If it does, however, the temporary withholding of information will be easily forgiven.

I had to take the *bus* to get here, which was as disgusting as always, but thankfully, I wasn't bothered by any miscreants or perverts. Now, I'm walking through the automatic doors of a department store, the same one that delivers our groceries each week in fact. This is the second time I've been here alone. The first was when I was looking for a gift for Anne. I knew they had an exclusive set of the little anime monster toys she collects here, and I wanted to surprise her with them. I didn't want to risk her finding them in the mail, so I needed to get them in person. I found them, thankfully, but I also found Marlon.

Marlon. *My brother*.

A woman in a red shirt and a green apron offers me a sample cup of some sort of cookie as

I walk past her little table. I shudder, thinking of when I was briefly human enough to almost have to eat. I shake my head no and walk faster.

The whole grocery area is useless to me, so I walk away from that third of the store and head toward home goods. When I see some of the anime monster trading cards on the way there, I consider stopping to get some for Anne but decide against it. If I get them, she'll know I went out and I'm trying to hide that.

Once at the home goods area, I look around near the bedding and it doesn't take long to spot him. Stocking the sheets and blankets is a tall, thin man with a shock of ginger hair, wearing the red shirt all the employees wear. He looks normal from far away, but I know if I get close enough to him, he'll look slightly off, just as I do.

"Hello, Marlon," I call out as I walk toward him.

When he looks up to see me, he smiles widely, his gap-toothed grin making him look friendly and approachable.

"Hi there, Ori! How's life?"

"Fantastic. Would be even better if I had the item you promised me, of course."

Marlon sighs and puts his freckled hands on his hips. "Straight to business then. No time to catch up with your only brother."

"Only brother that we know of, anyway."

It turns out I wasn't the only feather that fell off when the phoenix died. We think it was only two. Him, who ended up in a down comforter, and I. But we can't be sure.

"Oh, you. Well, I do have what you need. But you know as well as I do that it might very well be just garbage."

"I know that, brother. But I'll take any lead I can follow until I reach my destination. Don't worry about me."

"I have a feeling you can take care of yourself just fine," Marlon nods. "I'll be right back."

I wait for a few minutes, inspecting the low-quality pillows in this section before Marlon returns.

"Here you are. One map. I hope you can decipher the directions." He hands me a folded piece of paper that I take gladly.

"Thank you, Marlon. If this proves to be the real thing, I'll bathe you in riches, I promise." I shake his hand with a laugh.

"I don't need riches. I'm just happy to have found a brother. Come back and see me any time,

Ori."

"Of course."

Only if my plan succeeds, of course.

CHAPTER TWENTY-SEVEN

Carl

I'm so excited! I've never seen a cat up close, only through windows or on the internet. They look really soft and cute. Anne loves cats, so I'm happy she'll get time to play with them too. And of course, I'm excited just to be on a date. My very first date.

The café is bright and cheerful with art all over the walls depicting cartoon cats in all kinds of silly poses. There are shelves full of knickknacks for sale and more artwork on display. I pause on the way to the counter to inspect a particularly adorable statue of an orange kitten curled up on a big, white pillow. I'm going to have to bring that home to Ori for sure.

"Come on, silly goose. We can shop later. Let's get our drinks." Anne tugs my arm impatiently in the direction of the counter.

"Okay, okay." I laugh.

When we get to the counter, a smiling young person in a bright blue apron and matching blue hair greets us from behind the register.

"Hello, I'm Jamie. What can I get for you today?" They are incredibly peppy, and I have to wonder if everyone here is as upbeat as Jamie, if maybe working with cats is just that fun. Their colorful "they/them" name tag catches my eye, along with all of their flashy buttons. There is a smiley face button, one with a cute grumpy-faced cat, one supporting an ocean clean-up initiative, and more. I think I could be friends with Jamie.

"I'd like a matcha latte with soy, please. Oh, and one of those cupcakes shaped like a ball of yarn." Anne points inside a glass case containing various treats and I see a purple cupcake that has indeed been covered in tons of frosting strings made to appear as if it's a ball of yarn.

"I'll have, um…" I pause nervously.

I'm not very good at reading fast yet and some of these words on the menu I don't know. I start to feel really bad about myself. I've tried so hard to learn and I've done really well—I know I have. But some of these words are confusing. I don't want to seem stupid in front of a nice person. I know I'm not stupid, I'm just still learning. But it's hard to remember in times like this. Maybe I'll just order water, at least I know that.

"He'll have a green tea, unsweetened," Anne says.

I breathe a sigh of relief and smile at her, mouthing "thank you," when the server looks down to type in the order. I don't think I've ever had a green tea, but if she says I'll like, it I trust her. She's only truly led me wrong on beef and maple syrup. *Yuck.*

"Do you two have an appointment with the cats today?" Jamie asks.

We give them our appointment details and stand at the opposite end of the counter to wait for our goodies. It doesn't take long; Jamie seems to be very good at their job. We thank them and walk back to our table with the assurance that we'll be told when it's our time to visit with the kitties.

"Mmm, this is a good latte." Anne sips her drink with her eyes closed, clearly enjoying it. "We need to get out more."

I take a drink of my tea and flinch. "Ow! Hot!"

The tea was about a thousand degrees. I have no idea how Anne seems to be able to handle heat so well. She pats my hand while I blow on my tea and very carefully take another sip.

"Not so bad now that I can actually taste it." It's just some kind of plant water and that's fine with me.

"See? I knew you'd like it. Want to try some of my cupcake?"

"Yes, but I'll pass on the baked goods," I reply over the rim of my cup before taking another sip.

Anne nearly spits out her drink when she laughs at my innuendo. "Carl! Did you just flirt? And in a like perverted way?"

"It's not perverted. Oral sex is a very common practice between loving partners, Anne. Making a silly joke about wanting to lick your pu-"

"Oh my god, Carl, please stop," Anne begs as she sinks down in her seat, cheeks flaming red.

"I don't know why you're being weird but whatever, I'll stop. You should finish your treats because I think it'll be our time soon."

I was right. In only a few minutes we get called to go to the special room where the cats are. We're both finished so we walk in empty handed and ready for petting.

The room is cozy, with sofas, cat trees, and the like set up all around. There are toys all over to play with and I can't decide if I should grab one or just try to get a cat to play with me without one. Turns out I don't need to try to lure a cat to me, one just comes right over as soon as we take a seat on a big, gray sofa near the door.

"Hi kitty!" I whisper nervously when a large, black cat jumps onto my lap.

I'm afraid to touch it at first because I don't want to hurt it. It looks so small and fragile compared to me. But I take a chance, lower my hand to its sleek fur, and give it a long stroke. The cat crawls closer to me and butts its head against my chest, twirling around on my lap, then seeking out my hand again. What a strange creature. I pet it again and it begins to purr. I can't help but to grin so wide I feel like my face is going to split open when I hear that sound. *It's happy. I made it happy.*

"Oh, look at you! It likes you!" Anne squeals. "That's the most adorable thing I've ever seen."

The cat sniffs my hand and makes a sound like *mrow* before licking it. I laugh at the strange feeling. Its tongue is all bristly and weird and catches on the texture of my skin. It pauses to make that same sound again, then increases the pace of its licking.

A second cat hops onto the sofa and butts its head into my other hand. Anne, who is without cat, raises an eyebrow at me.

"Don't be jealous, I'm sure there will be one coming for you soon," I tease.

The second cat starts licking my hand even

more aggressively than the first one as a third cat begins to sniff my pant leg. A fourth jumps onto my lap, standing on its back legs to attempt to lick my neck. The one on the floor pushes its head under the hem of my pants and finds a sliver of bare leg where it begins to lick.

"Um, Anne, this is weird," I point out.

"Yeah, I don't think that's supposed to happen," she slowly replies as yet another cat joins the one on the floor in attempting to find leg skin.

Then, the one licking my neck takes a bite.

"Oh, fuck," I shout trying to push the cat away.

Unfortunately, the cats licking my hands grab tightly onto me with their paws and dig into my arms with their teeth. Anne screeches and attempts to help me, but they hiss and claw at her when she tries to get them off. Another cat jumps onto the back of my neck, digging its nails into my hair as it licks at me.

"Fuck fuck fuck," I repeat, trying to shake cats off of me.

"What the hell is going on?" comes a voice from the open door.

Jamie stomps into the room with a confused and unhappy look on their face. I much prefer the happy one.

"Get these cats off of me please," I plead.

"Why are they doing that? What did you do?" they bark at me accusingly.

"Nothing, I swear!"

"Bullshit. They only act this way when they get their Fishy Treats from the vet." They carefully pull a cat from my arm and walk it to a crate where they lock it safely inside. "The kind with the irresistible flavor, so they'll go where he wants them to. This is what you get for messing with them."

"I swear I didn't," I insist as Jamie continues to yank cats away from me and put them into crates.

"He really didn't," Anne chimes in.

"Whatever." Jamie really doesn't seem like they'll want to be my friend after this.

Anne just stays quiet, biting her lip, and rubbing my back soothingly while the whole ordeal ends. We're told not to come back and shown the door.

When we get outside, Anne looks at me with a grim expression as we walk to the car. Once we get inside, however, she bursts out in hysterical laughter.

"What?" I ask, confused. "That was not at all funny."

"It was. Don't you get what happened?" She continues to laugh so hard tears stream down her face.

"No. All I know is some cats decided to attack me."

"No. They decided you were a snack. I'm going to call you my Fishy Treat from now on." She breaks out in another round of laughter, and it finally hits me.

I guess you can't hide a fish from a cat.

CHAPTER TWENTY-EIGHT

Anne

I only need a quick shower after our trip and then I'm right back with Carl, alone in our apartment. Ori sent a text earlier that he'd be out for a bit so it's just us, and there's a feeling of anticipation as soon as I walk into the living room. He stands in front of the window, bathed in afternoon sunlight. He turns to me, and I see the deep yellow sun reflected in his bright blue eyes, a perfect ocean day. His golden skin shimmers and shines. His pale hair is wild from our misadventure at the café. When he smiles at me, his perfect white teeth flashing, he looks so youthful and healthy. I love this man. I *love* this man.

"Hey Carl. Doing okay?" is all my pea brain can think to say.

"Better than ever now that you're back. What do you want to do now?" His hands are behind his back and though he looks straight at me in a confident pose, there's something in the way his throat bobs and the pace of his breath increases that tells me he's as nervous as I am.

"Have a seat, Carl." I gesture toward the sofa.

"Uh, okay." He sits on the sofa with his hands at his sides, his posture perfectly straight.

Without hesitation I slink to the sofa as smoothly as I can, making sure to sway my hips along the way. I'm thankful I decided to wear a dress today. Normally I'm a practical pants type of woman, but I figured I'd stay dressed up for our date even after my shower. It's nice because when I get to Carl, I can hike my skirt up and straddle his thighs. The look on his face is absolutely priceless.

When I wrap my arms around his neck and settle myself on his lap, I see his eyes go wide, his mouth slightly open in awe. His cheeks have turned pink along with the tips of his ears.

"We have the place to ourselves, Carl. Let's take advantage of that," I purr.

"I think that sounds good," he shakily replies. "Can I touch you and stuff?"

"Absolutely. In fact, that's what I'm hoping for."

"Okay. Good."

There's a sudden change from shy boy to hungry man when his hands fly from his sides to my thighs, sliding up my dress to my hips and under the band of my underwear. He lifts his hips as he pulls me against him, forcing me to feel how hard he is for me. One hand slips back out and up behind my head pulling me toward him, joining us in a rough kiss that almost hurts my lips but more than anything feels so fucking good.

I roll my hips against him and moan into his mouth as he continues to kiss me deeply, passionately, gripping my hip, tugging at my hair. *Where has this Carl been?* He pulls my head away from his and looks into my eyes for a moment, breathing heavily, before speaking.

"Anne, I'm going to be forward with you. I would like to mate with you now. Would that be alright?"

He grips my hip tighter, as if he can keep me with him no matter my answer. His peculiar wording might make me laugh in another situation but right now it only makes me ache between my thighs.

"Yes, fuck yes. Mate with me, Carl. Take me, please," I beg.

His eyes are wild as he swings his arm under my ass and stands in one smooth motion. I yelp in surprise at the sudden change of position, but quickly calm as we head toward his bedroom.

Carl's bedroom is different from Ori's and mine. Where mine is filled on one side with all of Ori's business stuff and our gaming setup and anime collectibles on the other, Carl's is simple and the décor sparse. The only furniture is a bed, a side table with a lamp next to a soft chair he sits at to practice reading, and a dresser with a mirror and a photo of Ori and me on top of it. His possessions are all tucked away neatly and the only things on the walls are a couple pieces of my artwork. Everything is clean and dusted and he even makes his bed every day. *Such a good boy.*

With one hand Carl pulls aside the sheets and weighted blanket, then lays me on the bed. He stands over me, appraising, before placing a hand on either side of me and leaning down until his face is only inches from mine.

"I'm going to undress you now and then I'd like to taste you again. I'd appreciate it if you didn't try to stop me by acting all shy and stuff. Okay?"

I have to admit he's got me pegged. *Damn.* He really does pay too close attention to me, for real.

I nod. "Okay."

Carl nods back as he lifts my stretchy, sleeveless, yellow dress over my head. He tosses the dress on the floor and doesn't pause before sliding off my purple panties.

"Take off your bra, please," he requests as he stands to remove his own shirt.

I follow his directions and toss my bra to the side. He removes his shirt, rippling muscles appearing in front of me. *Fuck,* he looks amazing from all that swimming and running. As he unbuckles his belt, his eyes flick up and down my body, dark with lust.

"Spread your legs," he commands, forgetting the please this time, apparently, as he unzips his pants.

I almost get too shy to do as he says but remember his request from before and just swallow my awkwardness. I open my legs and hear the sharp intake of breath coming from him when his eyes meet my center. I take a few extra deep breaths of my own when he lowers his boxer briefs to reveal his thick, shimmering cock.

"You're very good at following directions, Anne. Normally, you're so stubborn." He laughs softly as he climbs onto the bed.

"What can I say? I'm hypnotized by lust."

"By lust? Hmm." He fits his shoulders between my legs, reaching a hand down and swiping a finger along my pussy. When he pulls his hand back I can see the glisten of my juices there.

"Definitely lust."

His head cocks to the side as he looks me in the eye for a moment. "Anne, when I'm desiring you and grow hard for a long time I feel an ache, sometimes it can feel almost really painful if I don't relieve it. Do you have that too? Do you ever desire me that way when you become wet like this? Is it the same as when I get hard?"

"This is a weird time for a question like that, but if you're asking if women get the equivalent of blue balls, then kind of? Yes, we can get so worked up that we can feel an ache where our clit is sort of and feel a sense of frustration. And yes, I've felt that way because of you before." My cheeks feel like they're going to burst into flames. "Why?"

"I'm just letting you know you can tell me any time, and I'll relieve your discomfort. Okay. That's all."

With that terrible segue, he drops down and lifts my ass at the same time. When his mouth meets my clit, his tongue swiping hard against it, I let out an embarrassingly loud moan of relief. My hands go to his hair and I direct him to all the places that need his tongue, his lips, his fingers.

He perfectly remembers every spot I've told him I like being touched, every movement, every type of pressure. "Memory of a goldfish" is clearly the most bullshit expression on the planet. It doesn't surprise me how very little time it takes for me to peak, shouting his name in pleasure.

He raises his head from between my legs, face wet and proud, and places a short kiss to my thigh.

"Thank you for that. I'm ready now," he says, surprising me.

"You're thanking *me?* I...okay. I'm not going to try to understand that one. Just come here."

I hold out my arms and when he meets me chest-to-chest it doesn't surprise me that our racing heartbeats beat in time with one another. Everything about us together, in this moment, is perfect.

"Mate with me, little fish," I whisper as our brows press together. "I need you inside me."

His breath quickens, his light hair tickles me, his pupils blacken the blue of his eyes. I'll remember every detail of this. I can feel the oh-so-slightly scaled texture of his cock, velvety soft in that place, as he rubs it up and down my wet slit, preparing to enter me.

"You'll take my seed then, Anne? You really want me? You're sure? I promise I'll be careful. I'll —"

"Carl," I stop him before he can go into a

panic, "just fuck me."

"Oh. Sure."

He starts slowly, pushing in gradually, a half an inch at a time. He keeps his eyes locked on mine the whole while and I can see a world of wonder in them. His eyelids flutter and his mouth pops open halfway through. When he's fully sheathed inside me, he groans, laying his head on my shoulder and letting out a long breath.

"Give me one second, Anne. Just one moment."

I can't help but giggle a little and pat him on the back. The only other person I've been with is Ori and he's not made of flesh, so it was much different. Oh, Ori. I hope he's alright. I hope—

"Oh, *fuck,* that feels good," I can't help but exclaim when Carl starts to slowly slide out of me. The texture on him, even though it's so light, somehow catches on my insides *just right.* "Holy fuck, Carl."

I wrap my legs around him when he is almost all the way out of me and shove him back inside. Needing more force from him. The muscles in Carl's strong arms shake then.

"Alright. That's how it will be then," he grits out between his teeth before pulling out of me and beginning to pound relentlessly back in and out again and again.

The drag of the texture on him through my insides at this speed and pressure is nearly unbearable. When he shifts so that my legs are pressed against my shoulders and he's grinding against my clit with every thrust, I explode in an orgasm so hard I think I see sparks, though I realize in my post-orgasm fog it's just the shimmer of his skin.

"Anne," he pants out, head dropping down to my neck, "I'm sorry, but I won't last much longer."

"That's okay, sweetie. I already came, and it feels so good. We can do it again as much as you want."

"I'm glad but...oh *fuck,* that feels so good. It's just that I don't know where your eggs are."

My brow furrows in confusion. "What?"

"Your eggs. Where did you put them so I can fertilize them? I don't think I can last much longer, you have to tell me. Oh my god. Anne, you feel amazing."

It hits me then that Ori did a terrible job of explaining human procreation to Carl and that even if he explained it to him that Carl doesn't know I'm on birth control. Holy fuck, this is a disaster. I'll just say...*shit*, what do I say? I'll make it easy, I guess.

"They're inside me, sweetie. That's how people do it."

"Oh. I like that then." Carl looks me in the eyes with a huge grin as his pace increases.

He leans down and kisses me hard, the kiss going wet, frantic, and so rough I think my lips will bruise until he shudders and slows, then stills. When he breaks the kiss and nuzzles his nose against mine that perfect feeling of connection returns for just a moment. I wipe the damp hair from his brow. He kisses down my neck as he lays next to me, arms around me, holding me tightly.

Then we hear the front door open and the moment is lost.

CHAPTER TWENTY-NINE

Ori

Home sweet home. I do hope my two had a lovely day. As I ride the elevator to our apartment, I wonder if they're home from the feline facility yet. The return visit on the bus took longer than I expected due to an incident involving a deviant in a trench coat harassing the driver and the police being called. Someday I will move my family out of this god forsaken city to somewhere more private. Somewhere with no *buses.*

When I enter the apartment, I can see the door to Carl's bedroom is open and the light is on. Both Carl and Anne are quite particular about turning off the light when they're not home so surely, they must be here. Seeing as it is the *only* light on, they must be in there together. *Success.*

Well, open doors in this house mean anyone can enter. I shove my hands in my pockets, trying and failing to reduce the width of my grin, and enter Carl's bedroom.

"Oh, hello there. And what have you two been up to? Here I thought you were out visiting a pussy café. Didn't know you'd decided for home brewed instead." The looks on their faces are priceless as I crack my admittedly crude joke. I'm not sorry, it was too easy.

"Ori, I'm going to kill you," Anne growls with a genuine look of frustration, or possibly even anger, on her face.

"It was only a joke. I'm fine with you fucking. Happy about it even. Congrats, by the way, Carl," I nod to the man, who is blushing dark red.

Carl buries himself farther under the sheet they've both covered themselves with and Anne's eyebrows form into an angry V. *What did I do?*

"I need to talk to you, Ori," Anne growls as she tosses off her half of the sheet. She picks up a yellow dress from the floor and a pair of purple panties, a pair I quite like, and jerks them on. "In the other room."

Still confused, I nod, and we head toward our bedroom. Anne stomps the whole way. When we get there, she shuts the doors so hard it could nearly be classified as a slam.

"Ori, I thought you told me you explained human reproduction to Carl. You encouraged me to be with him and when I was, he was missing crucial information."

"I explained to him how sex works and babies are made. You put the penis in the vagina.

To make a baby a sperm fertilizes an egg. I even explained oral sex, anal sex, where the clitoris is, all about my tentacles, what knotting is, what-"

"First off," I interrupt, "I don't know what knotting has to do with human reproduction. Second, and more important, you didn't tell him that the eggs aren't like fish eggs. That they aren't *outside*. And you know what? He didn't know anything about birth control. *Nothing*. Did you even explain safe sex to him? What if he'd have had sex with someone outside of this household and gotten a disease or gotten someone pregnant?"

A growl rises from my chest at the thought of Carl fucking anyone else. I bare my teeth as I snarl.

"Carl is *mine*. He would never take a lover outside of this house. *None* of us will. We will be together forever. Don't you understand, Anne? I will *never* let you go."

Anne's eyes widen and she backs away from me until the backs of her knees hit the bed. She stumbles backward and falls flat on her back. I lurch forward, planting my hands on either side of her face, my nose barely an inch from hers.

"Tell me you understand, Anne. My darling Anne." It's a plea and a command both.

"You're scaring me," she whispers. But I can

see her nipples harden under that dress. I can see how she licks her lips and squeezes her thighs.

"Tell me you know you belong to me, Anne. I've told you already I'm yours forever. I'll do anything for you, *be* anything for you. I live for and because of you. I could not have existed without you and now I *will not* exist without you. So, tell me you know. Say it. Say you're mine."

"I'm yours," she says in a voice that sounds like a whine and sigh at once, something reluctantly admitted but done with relief, nonetheless. "Forever."

I drop my nose the last inch to hers and sigh as the knock on the door breaks the tension.

"And so is Carl," I whisper before standing up. "Just...a little differently."

"Sorry, we had a disagreement, but everything is fine," I say as cheerily as possible when I open the door and see Carl's distressed visage behind it. "Do come in."

Carl enters the room wearing his favorite gray sweatpants and white tank top, looking like a fitness god compared to my long body in my black suit. We really are opposites and I'm pleased with my decision to make him so, though I wonder if he wouldn't have ended up with this build anyway. With his love of running and swimming he would be bound to end up somewhere in this direction at least.

And I know he would have loved Anne whether he received my feelings in my life force or not because his love is different from mine. I do see occasional glimpses of the possessive, rough, worshiping love I bring shine through, but his own love, the love at the front of it all, is all its own. Carl's love is quiet, curious, reverential. In the great series of luck I've had, he's one more four-leaf clover.

"Did I do something wrong?" he asks nervously, looking between Anne and me.

"Oh no. No, no. Here, sit with us," Anne says, patting the bed next to her. "I just was frustrated with Ori for not telling you about the eggs. And also, well, for not telling you that I can't get pregnant. At least not now, anyway. Are you upset?"

Carl heaves out a great sigh of relief and wraps his arms around the both of us as best he can in a hug before pulling away. There's a smile on his face that I'm quite happy to see.

"No way. I don't think I was ready for babies, but I was going to go for it anyway for you guys. And I'm glad about the egg thing because, wow, that felt really nice doing that inside of you, Anne." His cheeks go pink again and I can't resist poking at him. I just can't.

"That? You mean coming inside her? Filling her cunt with your hot—"

"Ori, stop!" Anne groans.

Carl looks away and I see him trying to slyly place a pillow over his lap, where an erection has become *very* obvious. I think now is the perfect time to bring up my ultimate plan.

"Speaking of filling my love with cum," I start.

"What a segue!" Anne throws her hands up in the air. I clear my throat.

"*Ahem.* You see, I can't. I can only produce feathers. It is a great tragedy. You, Carl, can. Now, as I am the alpha, it is my position to knot our omega. I've explained to you about knotting, yes?" I nod to Carl who nods back.

"Yes. The alpha expands at the base of his penis to create a firm hold inside the omega's vagina or anus and then the omega is pumped full of semen." Carl answers proudly.

"I'm going to die," Anne says, laying on her back with a pillow over her face. "We're discussing Omegaverse as if it's high school sex ed."

"Correct, Anne. You and I only moments

ago had a discussion on the importance of proper education so I'm simply making sure we're all on the same page. Now, back to the topic. I can easily create a knot with my abilities. That's beyond simple for me. Anne can take it, she's a champ."

"Thanks," she grumbles.

"You're welcome. What we're missing is the cum. That's where you come in, Carl."

"*Uuuugggggghhhh,*" Anne lets out a long, frustrated sound from under her pathetic pillow. I choose to ignore her at this moment.

"Quite literally *cum* in. You see, as my beta, you'll need to provide me with any assistance I require. In this case, I require your cock. We'll enter Anne together. We'll need to be careful of timing, of course, but you're good about following my directions so I trust you'll be able to wait until I'm ready." I pat Carl on the shoulder and I receive an awkward, confused grin in return.

"*Uuuuugggggghhhhhh.*" Anne again.

"We'll need a good amount of lubrication, and we'll need to take it slow. When I begin the knot, you'll be unable to move aside from perhaps the shallowest of thrusts, Carl, so you'll need to cum right before it's too late. The timing must be impeccable. Are we together on this?"

"Um. I'll do anything for you guys. And I

liked sex a lot when Anne and I tried it. So, I guess whatever you guys want," Carl replies, scratching the back of his neck and looking back and forth between the two of us.

"You're weird, Ori," Anne grouses, still under that unimpressive pillow.

"So that's a yes from all of us. Excellent! What a wonderful pack I have! Now we only need our omega to go into heat."

"People don't have heats." Anne sits up while rolling her beautiful eyes at me.

"We'll just have to make you beg for us then."

"I'm not going to beg to be double penetrated," she snorts.

"We'll see."

CHAPTER THIRTY

Carl

The awkwardness of that talk was a bit of a, uh, boner killer. So Anne and I left the room pretty quickly to get something to eat. The filling tacos we made hit the spot pretty well after the wild day. I had my first date, pet a cat, got attacked by a group of cats, got banned from a café, lost my virginity, officially entered a relationship, and got chosen to be part of a three-way Omegaverse sex thing. I'm not sure anyone has ever had quite a strange and busy day. Well, maybe Ori and Anne.

"Hand me your plate so I can put it in the dishwasher," Anne requests from behind me.

I've been done eating for a bit, but my mind has been wandering. As I raise my head to turn toward Anne with my plate in hand, I see Ori watching me closely over tented fingers across the table. *He's definitely plotting something.*

"Would you all like to watch a film?" He asks. *Here it goes.*

"Sure. What were you thinking?" Anne asks from near the sink.

"Oh, whatever you like darling. I would just enjoy some quality relaxation time with our little family. You've had such an exciting day."

"Sounds good. Hmm. There's this movie from like the eighties I think about a mermaid who gets legs and goes to New York to find a man she loves. Sometimes I think about Carl as a weird kind of merman. I mean, he's not, but with the whole scale-skin thing and being formerly a fish, you get the connection." She laughs. "It's a pretty funny and romantic movie so maybe we could watch that."

"I'd like that." I like that she thought of me when she thought of what movie to watch and it's kind of fun to be thought of as a merman as opposed to a weird fish-guy.

When we're all done in the kitchen, we head to our living room where we have a pretty nice setup. Our blue sofa is big and cozy. Ori doesn't really tolerate anything that isn't comfortable. We have all the streaming services and stuff because of Anne's anime addiction so we're able to find the movie she's searching for eventually. Anne sits to my left and Ori sits to my right and we start up the film.

It's kind of weird to have both Ori and Anne sitting next to me. Ori always sits next to Anne so I'm never in the middle. It feels weird at first like this, but then it feels nice. I feel safe and cared for. A weird fish-guy could get used to this.

The movie is really good and a few times Ori and I even chime in on how we can relate to some things, like the fear of getting caught as a non-human, or how strange it is getting used to things humans are already so used to. When the bad guys catch the mermaid though, it makes me feel kind of nervous. It hits a little too close to home. I'm always afraid that someday someone will discover Ori or I and take us away and hurt us.

"You seem tense, Carl," Ori observes.

"A little," I reply quietly, trying not to disturb Anne, who is super engrossed in the movie.

"Let me rub your shoulders then," he offers.

"Sure, that sounds nice." It does sound great. With all the swimming and stress and excitement, my muscles are pretty tight.

I angle my body to give Ori better access and he begins to rub, doing it just how I like: slow and hard.

"Does that feel alright, Carl?" Ori asks quietly.

"Definitely." I sigh, letting some of the stress go.

"Here, let me get some lotion and you can take off your shirt. It will be even better, hmm?" Ori purrs next to my ear.

Hmm. Now he seems suspicious. But… *massage.* I can't resist.

"Okay," I reply as I lift off my shirt and tuck it next to me on the sofa.

A few seconds later, I feel hands slathering my skin with lotion before they return to rubbing away my stress. Where he got the lotion in the living room, I have no idea, but I don't take the time to wonder. Instead, I close my eyes and let out a grateful moan as I feel a knot in my muscles come loose.

A sharp inhale of breath from in front of me makes me open my eyes. Anne is watching us, eyes focused where Ori's fingers are sliding over my skin. When she briefly looks up at my face and notices me watching her, she snaps back toward the screen without a word.

"Let me get a little on your lower back. You look a bit tight there as well," Ori says.

"Yeah, sounds good," I whisper back, eyes on Anne to see if she reacts.

When Ori begins to work a sore spot near my hip, I can't help but release a groan. Anne's eyes flit to the side to watch again, but she looks away once more as if guilty of something. When I let out a strained "Fuck," at Ori's manipulation near my spine her eyes linger longer. Her little pink tongue darts out to lick her lips and I can't help but start to grow hard in my sweatpants. *Damn, I hope Ori doesn't get weirded out by that.*

Ori is very much *not* weirded out by that.

"Oh, how tense you are. Perhaps we can alleviate this discomfort as well?" Slowly he slides a hand around my hip, across my pelvis, and under the waistband of my pants.

I hiss and jerk my hips in surprise as his fingertips make contact with my stiff cock. This, of course, gets the attention of Anne, whose jaw drops all the way when she sees what's going on. She freezes in place, silent, and stays that way as Ori continues.

"So incredibly tense that even the softest touch makes you jump. *Tsk.* How poorly we've taken care of you these past months." Ori drags a lotioned palm down the length of my cock and then cups my balls, squeezing them gently. "You need a release, beta."

When I try to reply all that comes out is heavy breathing. *This is so weird.* When Ori wraps his hand around my shaft and starts to stroke me, I can't help but to thrust my pelvis along with him. The texture of his hand is so strange and the way it runs against the semi-scaled texture of mine, slippery with whatever he's using as lotion, is maddening.

"Please," Anne breaks her silence.

"What's that, Anne?" Ori asks before giving my cock this incredible twisting-squeeze-twirl motion that has me groaning loudly. He snaps his teeth against my earlobe. "Ssh, dear, Anne has something to say to us."

"Please. I give in. The fucking. I'll beg. This is just too much." Her voice is breathy and quick, as if she can't get the words out fast enough.

"Say 'Please fuck me at the same time. I want both of your cocks inside my cunt.'" Ori's words and his stroking are almost too much for me, but I have a feeling I'm not supposed to cum now. *Damn it.*

"Please fuck me with both your cocks in my pussy at once or whatever you said. Oh my god, just hurry," Anne whines.

Ori *cackles* and releases me from his grip. I let out a deep sigh and slump forward. *Here we go.* This day just keeps getting weirder.

CHAPTER THIRTY-ONE

Ori

I knew it would work. There are few anime fans who like the things Anne does who can resist the allure of two exceptionally handsome men at once. I've seen the hentai she watches. I've read the manga and the fan fiction she reads. If she thinks I don't know what will please her, then she's forgotten the most important thing about me: that I will do *anything* to make her happy.

And now I'll do whatever it takes to make Carl happy as well. If someone had asked only half a year ago if I'd ever care for anyone even half as much as Anne, I'd have torn the life from them for even suggesting such a thing. How quickly things can change.

Of course, Anne will always be my first priority. She is part of me. The first flickers of my life were given to me by her. I would not exist without her, and I exist for her. But now it's only...I have someone else to live for as well. Someone else I look forward to seeing every day. Someone I... well, *love*, in the way that I'm able to. How strange life is.

I carry Anne to our bedroom bridal style

and lay her on our bed. She's let her hair grow out a little in the last few months. Not much, of course; she still hates attention and lovely hair like hers would surely draw looks were it to grow long. Right now, it spreads around her in a golden-brown halo on the bedspread, framing her face, so full of lust.

The corner of my lip lifts in a taunt. "My sweet Anne, so full of desire, with such an empty cunt. It will only be but a moment, my love. Do not despair."

Anne spreads her legs and slips a hand into her panties, beginning to fondle herself. "Hurry, Ori. I need you."

I panic momentarily. When my Anne says she needs me I react instinctually. My head swivels to the doorway where thankfully I find Carl waiting, leaning against the doorframe, arms crossed over his well-built chest.

The bulge in Carl's pants is exceptional and impossible to ignore, but I tear my eyes away. His pants fall low on his hips, showcasing his Adonis belt, the V-shaped line running from his hip bones to under said pants. His abdominal muscles are well-defined, his shoulders and arms strong. The light hits on the angles of his face, making the scales on the high parts of his cheekbones shimmer. Despite the sharp jawline and his deeply masculine appearance, he still looks youthful, curious, sweet. Perfect for Anne. And I wonder if somehow, I didn't subconsciously make him a little bit for me as well. Or perhaps that developed over time. Maybe it's nothing and I'm just overthinking things at the moment.

I could tear my hair out thinking of all of this...*emotional* business, but I have important things to focus on. Things such as Anne and the orgasms we're all about to have. Good. That will get my mind off of things.

"Come on now, Carl. You heard the woman. She needs us." I snap.

"I don't know," he drawls, inspecting his nails. "She said she needs you. She didn't say anything about me."

Damn it.

Anne shoots up and turns to face Carl. "I need you both. Now. Please." she whines.

Carl breaks out in that boyish grin of his and leaps onto the bed, tackling Anne. They both break out into raucous laughter. *Perfect.*

"What a silly omega and beta I have," I purr as I begin to remove my clothes. "If you want to play together, then why don't you race to see who can undress the fastest."

Anne wins by a mile.

"Totally not fair. Pants are harder to take off than dresses," Carl complains as he lays on the bed, nude, one arm behind his head, one leg up.

"You snooze, you lose." Anne snarks from next to him. She's laying on her side, facing me, head propped on her hand.

Looking at the two of them laying there in their fully naked glory I could nearly feather myself by the time I'm undressed. Damn all these layers of clothes I wear.

Finally, I'm down to nothing but my fabric skin. I slink onto the bed to meet my mates, wrapping an arm around the both of them, pressing my body against Anne's.

"Are you in heat, my omega? Do you need my knot to fill you?"

"Yes. Yes, alpha," she replies from right next to my ear. I growl. *Finally,* she's playing along.

"First, I need you to cum. Get on Carl's face," I bark out an order.

Carl shakes his head in confusion at the same time Anne pulls away.

"I can't do that! I'll suffocate him!" Anne squeals.

"I'll hold you up. I'd never let Carl die. Besides, he's a fish, he's used to breathing in fluids. Now, Carl? You're ready?"

"Absolutely," he grins. I know him too well.

Anne bites a lip nervously but straddles his face, nonetheless. I hold her hips gently, ready for if she needs me, and smile as she lowers herself onto him.

She doesn't stay shy for long, and I don't have to hold her hips. Carl grabs onto her ass like it's the only thing keeping him from drowning in a sea of pussy and presses her harder against him rather than keeping her farther away. Anne certainly doesn't try to be gentle with him. The way she grinds on him reminds me of when she flattened my face and I have to let out a quiet laugh as I stroke myself alongside them.

Then I sneakily laugh again as I decide to stroke Carl as well. He nearly bucks the two of them off the bed in surprise, but to his credit, doesn't stop feeding on her cunt like he does it for a living. In fact, I think the extra motion finally sets her off and she cums against him, squeezing her thighs around his head. Finally when she's panting and done, she rolls off of him. He lets out a gasp for air and I let go of his cock.

"There we are. We're all ready then." I reach

over to the side table and grab the bottle of lubricant. "Time to play."

CHAPTER THIRTY-TWO

Anne

Easy enough for these two to be relaxed about this, but they aren't the ones about to be double stuffed. Well, as nervous as I am, *fuck* I want it bad.

I turn back to Carl and place my hand on his cheek, bringing his face to mine for a deep kiss as I swing my leg over him. I've thought about the logistics of this...a lot...and I think this position will be the best. So, when Carl holds my ass and drags my soaking wet slit along his cock, I reach down and line it up with my cunt. Sinking down onto his textured skin feels nice but raising up on it feels just as weird and amazing as it did earlier. I'm seriously the luckiest woman on the planet, hands down.

"Lean forward a bit more, darling," a raspy request comes from Ori. I obey his command and a hiss comes from behind me. "Look at you two. My naughty darlings joined together. Perfect."

The sound of a cap popping open, followed by a good amount of liquid being sloshed around, joins the sound of Carl and I making love. Soon, some of that liquid is rubbed onto and into me by

Ori's soft hands. I can feel him rub some onto Carl and hear him slather it onto himself.

Ori takes hold of my hips as he drops a leg over both of Carl's. "Be still for a moment. Breathe and keep your muscles relaxed. I'll start small."

Ori keeps his promise and doesn't enter me too large, though his ego prevents him from going too small. The stretch of him entering me with Carl already inside burns at first but Ori is slow, checking in to make sure I'm okay with every little bit. I keep my eyes focused on Carl, who has his hands on my hair, stroking it and alternating kisses with sweet words.

"You're doing so good, Anne. That feels crazy, right?" Carl smiles and nudges his nose against mine. "You're such a crazy girl. I love you so much."

A tear forms at the corner of my eye. *How dare he tell me he loves me when I'm being double penetrated.* But yet it's still somehow perfect.

"I love you too," I force out as Ori sinks another inch inside me.

Carl's smile is so wide I don't know how I'll ever manage to kiss all of it, but I do. The kiss is wonderful. The fresh, clean taste of his tongue, the texture of his face that's become so familiar to me against my hand, the brush of soft hair against my cheek, it's all perfect. Even the moans we let into each other's mouths when Ori finally fits fully inside me and begins to rock in and out are perfect.

I break the kiss and toss my head back to let out a long groan of pleasure. Now that the initial stretch is over, everything feels so, so good. I feel full like I've never felt before and I know the feeling is only going to increase when Ori really starts his little game.

Carl starts to find his groove opposite Ori and I'm too overwhelmed to say anything or do anything other than just be fucked. I'm completely at their mercy and for once I don't mind losing control a little.

Ori pulls me against his chest and both men adjust their positions to accommodate. Dark hair brushes my cheek as he nips my ear. "Look at my Anne, fucked by two men at once. Pathetically mewling and desperate on our cocks. Do you want to be knotted, my desperate little omega? Do you want to be stuffed with cum until it leaks down your thighs, drenches the sheets? Answer yes and maybe I'll even let you cum too."

A sob is wrenched from my chest. I don't know if I can speak right now, I'm so overwhelmed. But I'll try. A high-pitched noise comes out, that's it. I try again.

"Yes," I breathe out. "Knot me. Fill me."

Another sob is all I can manage after that, but it seems good enough for Ori. I feel him begin to grow inside me, larger all around but even larger still at the base.

"Faster Carl. It's time," he snaps as he bends me.

Carl sits up more so that we're all close to one another in every way. He begins thrusting up into me rapidly, leaning in to kiss me wet and messy. Ori continues to slowly grow until both Carl and I pull away from one another, gritting our teeth.

"I can't...I can't last any longer," Carl looks over my shoulder at Ori. Whatever look Ori gives Carl has him nodding and going as fast as he can against Ori's increasing size.

He keeps his eyes on Ori and, to my surprise, when he cums he reaches a strong hand out and pulls Ori's face to his, trapping him in a brutal kiss. *Well hello.*

CHAPTER THIRTY-THREE

Carl

Ori's tongue feels strange. Not like Anne's. But I like it. All of Ori feels different. I like that we're all different. We're all special. It makes things twice as fun.

And *holy shit, I'm kissing Ori. What am I doing?*

As the last drops of cum are spurting out of me, the base of his cock swells so thick I can't move anymore. It kind of makes me want to panic, because who wouldn't panic when their cock was trapped, but I trust him. He gave me life, after all.

I break the kiss and look into his eyes, desperate for an answer to my unspoken question: *"Was that okay?"*

Ori's eyebrows are raised in surprise and his wet mouth is open in shock. My hand is still on the back of his head, and I can't help but to give his scalp a soothing scratch. His bright eyes flutter closed, and his face relaxes. He tips his head to mine until our foreheads touch, giving me my answer: "*Yes, it was.*"

"*Fuck!*" Anne shouts from between us and my attention snaps back to her.

"Are you okay, pretty girl?" I ask.

"I'm so stretched out. I don't know if I can take it any longer." She grips my biceps and bites down on my shoulder when Ori shifts his hips. Her blunt teeth and gentle bite don't hurt but I worry she's not having a good time and I want to stop if she's not.

"Anne, we've practiced with my tentacles. You've got this." Ori swipes her hair across her shoulder and kisses her cheek. "The fun is really just beginning."

"Oh, wasn't that the end?" I ask with a cock of my head.

"Oh no. We have to *fill her* with cum. Once isn't enough." Ori pats me on the cheek then returns to holding Anne steady. "And don't worry about the next round. I've got you."

"What does that mean?" I'm very genuinely confused now as Anne breathes a laugh against my chest.

"We love surprise tentacles in this house," she giggles. "Say no if you're opposed though."

"I...don't think I am?" I guess I'll say no if I figure out what the hell they're talking about and don't like it.

"Excellent." Ori scrapes his teeth over Anne's shoulder causing her to moan against my chest.

Just then I feel something tickle against me as Anne moans more and more. With us sandwiched together like this I can't see what's going on down there but whatever it is Anne sure seems to like it.

"What's going on?" I brush her hair behind her ear and moan softly myself as she ripples inside around Ori and me.

"Tentacles." Ori laughs darkly as he places a finger under my chin, lifting my face to his. "Surprise."

It's then that I feel them begin to squirm around me. They slither from Ori, squeezing along my shaft while it's still trapped inside Anne, wrapping around my sac, and sliding along the passage that leads to my rear entrance. My cheeks turn hot, and I tense up when I realize what he's planning on doing.

"It's thin and lubricated and if you relax it won't hurt you. Quite the opposite. Just ask Anne." Ori nips her earlobe and she groans, but in delight.

"Oh, fuck yes. Kiss me, Carl." Anne begs and I can't resist her, I can't resist anything Anne asks of me.

Anne presses her mouth hard against me, licking and sucking on my lips desperately. The wet tentacles around my balls start massaging in the strangest ways, rippling, squeezing, pulsing. It shouldn't feel as good as it does, but combined with the way Anne is clenching inside and the little bit I can thrust it's fucking glorious. And then when I relax, the tentacle breaches my asshole, swells just slightly, and hits a pleasurable spot I never knew existed, I'm panting right along with Anne.

The tentacles that are working on Anne begin to move faster and soon she's crying out and shaking in an orgasm. *Fuck, she's so beautiful.* She's sweating and her hair is stuck to her face, but she looks like she's in ecstasy.

All the slippery tentacles on and in me work faster, their strange motions confusing and exciting me and I don't even care what they're doing, I just know it feels fucking fantastic. My hips thrust faster in the shallow movements I'm able to make and everything is so warm, so wet. Anne's head is on my shoulder, her lips softly caressing my neck. Ori's eyes are locked on mine as I cum again.

When I'm done and feel like I'll scream if I'm touched anymore, Ori suddenly retracts all the tentacles, except for the one behind me, which he removes more slowly.

"Anne, Carl, lie back. I need to see this." His voice is rough and desperate, and I remember that tone from when I was in the tank. *He's close.*

Anne and I lie back as Ori begins to shrink inside her, watching the point where we're all joined with complete focus. When he's back to a normal human size, and Anne is bent over, he slides out of her. I can feel both our combined liquids rush out of her and over my legs. Ori's eyes open wide, and his grin goes manic as he takes in the sight.

"Yes, that's it. That's what I wanted to see. You did so well, both of you."

Anne and I both just lie there and pant as Ori spouts feathers onto the cum, making it a three-person mess.

"I need a bath," Anne mumbles from beside my ear.

I can't help but laugh as I agree that I need the same.

"I'll start the water," Ori offers as he hops up and off to the bathroom.

"Come on, Anne. I've got you," I say once I'm sure my legs will be steady.

I pick her up and carry her to the bathroom where Ori has started the water just like he said he would. When I sit in it with her in front of me, she sighs.

"Exactly what I needed. I think I'm going to be sore for a week. At least." She snuggles back against me and I wrap my arms tightly around her.

Ori sits on a stool next to the tub with a pile of clean towels on his lap. Somehow in the last minute he got himself cleaned up and I have no idea how.

"Ori, how did you just get clean so fast?"

"It's private."

"What? Why?"

"Everyone needs a secret, even if it's a little one."

"Boo," Anne says sleepily with a thumbs down.

I laugh. "Agreed. Boo."

"Boo or not, I have your towels and I'm going to sit here and relax until you're done. I have to make sure the people I love don't fall asleep in the bathtub and drown."

"The people you love, huh?" I try to ask lightly but my throat feels like it's closing up. This feels like a big deal, and I need to hear it again.

"Yes. I love you both." He turns away and inspects his nails, putting an arrogant look on his face. "So, you're quite lucky of course. Having someone so loyal, dedicated, handsome, tentacled, no wonder you love me so much."

His eyes shoot to the side and there is a hint of vulnerability there.

"It's no wonder we love you indeed," I assure him.

"The tentacles really seal the deal," Anne mumbles.

We all laugh. The rest of the night is spent in relaxation until finally I'm able to get some sleep. What a weird day that was.

The next morning at breakfast, Ori sits at the end of the table watching the two of us eat our cereal.

"So," he says, crossing his arms primly in front of him. "Now that we did Omegaverse and that's over with-"

"That's over with already?" Anne asks with

a raised eyebrow.

"Yes, of course. As I was saying, now that that's over with, what shall we try next? Anne, any ideas? Carl?" He looks back and forth between Anne and I as the two of us just look confused. "Come on now, there are masses of things to play. Some are more difficult. 'Mpreg' or 'why choose?' wouldn't be possible for our dynamic, for example."

"Ori. No more fan fiction." Anne drops her head to the table, making a loud thump.

"We'll see. We could always find ways to set up a pretend alternate universe. I could temporarily gender swap, I think anyway. Alternate setting trope. Unexpected baby. Damsel in distress. Partner-"

"Ori. Let's just be normal for a little bit, okay? Carl hasn't even had a single day of being in a normal relationship. We should just have no surprises, no games, no fanfic."

"How long do I have to be normal?"

"What?" Anne asks incredulously. "You want a specific date?"

"Yes. When can I surprise you?"

"Well, I guess Christmas is the closest date where surprises are expected." Anne chuckles.

"You better not 'unexpected pregnancy' me though. Hard limit."

"Oh, I have something else in mind."

CHAPTER THIRTY-FOUR

Anne

A few months after that heaping help of stuffing, we've settled into our routine. We work, we relax, we even leave the house sometimes. We just tend to avoid the mall and cat cafes. Everything is wonderful.

Today is Christmas and we're settled in front of our little tree opening gifts. I'm not great at picking out gifts, and we told each other we wouldn't get anything expensive, so I didn't get them anything super big. I just hope they like what I got them anyway.

Ori tears into the perfectly wrapped gift I know is from me with total glee in his eyes. He pulls out a thick book and a sheet of paper.

"Oh, Anne, I love it! I'm going to learn all about the overlords. We'll have power soon, you'll see."

I scrunch my brow. Overlords? *What's he talking about?* I know he's been talking about wanting to learn about politics, but not knowing where to begin, so I got him signed up for a community education introduction to American politics class. I also got him a book on the history of America as told from a variety of ethnic and immigration viewpoints. I figure once he gets all that down, he can move onto world politics. This overlord stuff is weird though. Then again, it's Ori. Who knows with him? I just smile and look at Carl, who is opening his package from me.

"Whoa, look at all these!" he exclaims when he sees what's in the package I got him.

He has been super dedicated to learning to read, and he's great at it now. Reading is basically his favorite hobby. I tried to get him to read the manga I like, and Ori tried to get him to read fanfic, but he wasn't interested. So, I thought I'd try giving him something I'm pretty sure he'll be into. And, if not, at least it's silly enough for him to smile.

"Okay, what's this one?" He picks up the first book and reads the blurb on the back. "This is about a...sentient *door*? And it's a romance?"

"What can I say, I got you some books that reminded me of you two. I think you'll like them." I bite my lip to keep myself from laughing.

He picks up the next one. "This is a swamp creature romance? And this next one is a living Jack-in-the-Box? A scary house that comes alive! Anne!"

Carl stares at me with the books in his hands. *Uh-oh*. Maybe I made a mistake, and he hates them.

"I love them!" He grins and looks at all the covers again, running his hands over them, rereading the blurbs.

"Let me know what you think of them."

"My turn, my turn," Ori interrupts. "I can't wait. I've waited months for this surprise."

I sigh and cross my arms. *Here we go*. As long as it's not a surprise pregnancy we should be fine. Ori hands us each an envelope and steps back, bouncing on his toes in excitement.

"Okay. Here we go." I look at Carl as we both open our envelopes.

At the same time, we each pull out...a map. *Huh?* I hold the map in front of me looking for any sign of what it might mean or where the map even leads but can't figure it out.

"So, what is this?" Carl asks.

"Glad you asked," Ori says as he steeples his hands under his chin. "For the past half a year or so I've been researching the most important topic in the world. I'm sorry that I've had to hide what I've been doing but if my plan had failed I didn't want to disappoint you. Thankfully, I have not failed.

"Not only did I accidentally discover a way to permanently renew myself when we offed those security guards, I also found out I have a brother, and I discovered the natural habitat of the phoenix, which is what is marked on your map.

"Most importantly, I discovered what is almost surely the solution to the problem we have."

"We have a problem?" I ask.

"Yes, a very big one."

"And what's that?"

"You and Carl will die and I will not."

"Well, that's morbid," I grumble.

"And you can't really fix that," Carl chimes in.

"No, Carl. Humans can't fix that. *I* can."

Carl and I give each other another confused look as Ori gets down on one knee in front of us, pulling a small box from his front pocket.

"Anne. Carl. We have an adventure to go on."

With a nervous clearing of his throat, he opens the box to reveal a tiny flame.

"That is, if you want to live forever."

Afterword

Thanks for reading Double Stuffed! I hope you enjoyed reading it as much as I loved writing it. It was tons of fun to bring Carl into the picture and give Ori and Anne someone else to interact with who wasn't an enemy, since they didn't really have anyone else in Stuffed. They sure did interact too, wowza.

When I write I don't plan anything out really. I come up with the general idea ("I'm going to write a sequel to Stuffed because people want me to" was all I really had for this, for example) and just start writing. I had no idea what was going to happen so I was as surprised as anyone else by what was going on in each scene. It's a really fun way to write, even if things can get a bit chaotic. I really did not expect Ori and Carl to fall for each other the way they did. In fact, I was pretty dead set against it from the start. But they just wanted to be together so it happened and I'm happy it did.

Now, about the ending...will I write a third one? I don't know. The ending is more for fun and just imagining the things that could happen. If enough people wanted a third maybe I could write it, but otherwise I'll just leave it up to the "what ifs" that it can create.

Oh, one more thing! In the book Carl

receives a gift of books from Anne. I based those descriptions on real books you might enjoy if you liked this one. Here they are:

Unhinged by Vera Valentine (the door book)

Seduced By the Swamp Creature by Ivanna Schloppykoch (the swamp creature book)

Jacked Up by Latrexa Nova (the Jack-in-the-Box book)

They Came From the Walls by S.R. Griffith (the house book)

Thank you again for reading my book and I hope you'll check out more from me. Stay firm and cool!

Check Out My Recent Book, Goat Girl!

He said he'd never met a mashie until he fell for me.

Superheroes are real. Unfortunately, so are supervillains, and one turned me into a goat girl.

Since The Big Mash-Up things have been pretty tough for us mashies, or those who got stuck being half animal. I lost my home and my dreams. Now I'm working minimum wage, dealing with a public that sometimes wishes I didn't exist.

And then he walks into my life.
The sexiest man who's ever ordered a drink from me.
Liam Jemison.

An entomologist working to help solve lingering issues from The Mash-Up, he tells me I'm the most beautiful woman he's ever seen. His kisses make me feel like I'm on fire and every touch has me aching for more. He says he wants me and likes everything about me. It feels real but can I risk trust in a world like this?

Can I believe in heroes when the world treats me like a villain?

Find it today on Amazon!

Printed in Great Britain
by Amazon